Read July 8/1993
Tony d'Gregan

THE ABBÉ TIGRANE

Ferdinand Fabre

THE ABBÉ TIGRANE

*Translated from the French
and with an Introduction by*

ROBERT LIDDELL

PETER OWEN · LONDON

ISBN 0 7206 0693 4

Translated from the French *L'Abbé Tigrane, Candidat à la Papauté*

PETER OWEN PUBLISHERS
73 Kenway Road London SW5 0RE

First published in Great Britain 1988
English translation © Peter Owen Ltd 1988

Photoset by Ann Buchan (Typesetters) Shepperton
Printed in Great Britain by
A. Wheaton & Co. Ltd Exeter

Introduction

Ferdinand Fabre (1827–98) was at one time regarded as the founder of the French regional novel, but he died just when his election to the French Academy was certain, and his fame seems to have declined ever since. Nevertheless, his first novel, *Les Courbezon* (1862), met with immediate success: it was crowned by the French Academy, and Sainte-Beuve in his review called the author 'the strongest of the disciples of Balzac'. In the years that followed he published some twenty novels; he has been called 'the Hardy of the Cevennes', his country of predilection. Several times he wrote 'Scenes of Clerical Life' – nearer to Trollope than George Eliot though not near to either, for his priests are not country gentlemen, and in *Tigrane* no important character is a layman. After 1883 he became curator of the Mazarin Library. Renan had admired him and, above all Taine, who said that his novels were essential reading for anyone who wished to study the history of France in the nineteenth century. Walter Pater (who published an enthusiastic essay on Fabre in 1901) well defined his subject-matter: 'The passions he treats of in priests are, indeed, strictly clerical, most often their ambitions – not the errant humours of the mere man in the priest, but movements of spirit properly incidental to the clerical type itself.'*

Three years later Edmund Gosse (who had caught the enthusiasm from Pater) made an important study of him, yet neither he nor Pater seems to have had any success in introducing Fabre to English readers. Gosse gives us a clue to the neglect of this author whom he so much admired: '. . . the novels of Ferdinand Fabre have one signal merit: they are entirely unlike those of any other writer; but they have one equally signal defect – they are terribly like one another. Those who read a book of his for the first time are usually delighted, but they make a mistake if they immediately read another.'

* Reprinted in *Essays from the Guardian* (London, 1910).

L'Abbé Tigrane, Candidat à la Papauté (The Abbé Tigrane, Candidate for the Papacy), first published in 1873, is universally recognized as Fabre's best work. Gosse, who unhesitatingly placed it among the best European novels for some thirty years, read it 'with rapture' and reread it with 'undiminished admiration'. His verdict may still be accepted: 'On one solitary occasion the author of very pleasant, characteristic and notable books, which were not quite masterpieces, shot up into the air and became almost a writer of the first class.'*

This book, lent to me at Oxford more than fifty years ago by my friend Vere Somerset of Worcester College, has remained at the back of my mind ever since, and in the intervening years I made many unsuccessful attempts to get hold of a copy. Finally, I reread it in 1986, like Gosse with 'undiminished admiration', despite certain *longueurs*: the hysteria of the principal character is at times exhausting, and often a series of discourses replaces dialogue. But the story is riveting.

The main action of the plot takes place in 1866, not in Fabre's Cevennes but at Lormières, a fictitious small cathedral city somewhere between Toulouse and Perpignan – a city with religious establishments up on a hill, and paper-mills down by the little river. The hero (or villain) of the book is the Abbé Rufin Capdepont, Superior of the Great Seminary and Canon of the cathedral of St Irenaeus. He was a peasant from the Spanish frontier who came as a scholarship boy to the Great Seminary, where his tigerish ferocity when fellow students mocked him for his uncouthness earned him the nickname 'Tigrane'. His striking intelligence and industry marked him out for an important future, and caused him to cherish ambitions – the priesthood (conferred on him when he was twenty-five) limited these to the clerical world, and he was determined to become a bishop, a prince of the Church. He interested the Baron Thévenot, a *nouveau-riche* paper manufacturer ennobled by Louis-Philippe and a deputy, who took Capdepont to Paris as tutor to his son, and there he made influential friends. Thévenot, however, had a political débâcle, and Capdepont returned to the Great Seminary where (under a weak bishop, Mgr Grandin) he soon dominated the diocese which he hoped presently to rule. Here he had

* *French Profiles*, Collected Essays, vol. IV (London, 1913); first printed 1904.

6

one ally and confidant, a former fellow student, the Abbé Mical, a mean, devious person who hoped to rise in the world with his brilliant friend – whose violence he did his utmost to restrain. In 1855 Mgr Grandin died, and Capdepont worked furiously in Paris to be elevated to the vacant see, but it was bestowed on the Marquis Armand de Roquebrun, Canon of Arras, whom Capdepont henceforth hated with bitter jealousy.

Mgr de Roquebrun was in many ways the opposite of Capdepont: he was a nobleman from the North with exquisite courtly manners – ultramontane, as deeply attached to the Holy See as Capdepont was to the Gallican movement in favour of increased independence of the French Church. The Bishop's supporters were the Abbé Ternisien, his private secretary, a weak but holy man, a Franciscan whom he had brought from Rome; also the old noble families, headed by the Vicomte de Castagnerte, and the poor in the Quarter of the Paper-Mills, to whom he was boundlessly generous. His generosity, however, was not confined to Dickensian benevolence, but largely consisted in organized charity (hospitals, schools, etc.) in alliance with the religious orders, now returned to France, which did not endear him to Capdepont and the diocesan clergy. He had also antagonized local patriotism by an extensive liturgical reform, getting rid of most of the feasts peculiar to the diocese of Lormières, and in consequence giving the calendar a more international (or perhaps one might say more Roman) appearance.

On arriving at Lormières Mgr de Roquebrun had done all he could to win Capdepont to himself, but the obstinate Superior of the Great Seminary returned only formal thanks for any favours his bishop obtained for him, treating him with insolence and defying him on every possible occasion. Moreover, the Bishop feared that his Gallicanism verged on heterodoxy and regretted that he should be responsible for the training of future priests. After ten years at Lormières he resolved (a somewhat authoritarian action) to transfer Capdepont and the other directors of the Seminary to different posts in the diocese, and to replace them by members of a religious order. 'At last, after a wild encounter, his (Capdepont's) insolence brings on an attack of apoplexy in the Bishop, and the hour of success or final failure seems approaching. But the Bishop recovers, and in a scene absolutely admirable in execution contrives to turn a public ceremony, carefully prepared by Capdepont to humiliate him, into a

7

splendid triumph!' * The Bishop, who had hoped Capdepont would sufficiently disgrace himself to put his succession to the bishopric out of the question, fears Mical may restrain him, and forms another plan: he will ask for Ternisien to be made coadjutor or suffragan, to help him in his feeble state of health, for then his succession will be almost a matter of course. He takes him to Paris, but there dies in a second apoplectic fit.

Capdepont is now mad with anxiety and ambition. When Ternisien returns with the body of the dead bishop, Capdepont (temporarily the chief authority in the diocese) in his hatred refuses to admit it to the cathedral. There follow the strongest and most dramatic scenes in the book. Roquebrun's coffin lies in the court of the bishop's palace, and later on the steps of the cathedral, deluged with rain during a terrible thunderstorm, guarded by Ternisien and other loyal priests of the diocese, and by the religious orders, who with difficulty open the cathedral after nightfall and perform the office for the dead. Next day, after the end of the dirge and the requiem, and after they have laid the coffin with the former bishops in the crypt, Capdepont appears in St Irenaeus. He is coldly received, for the clergy now believe Ternisien will be the next bishop (little as he desires it). But Capdepont reveals that he has been nominated by the Emperor, and nearly everyone flocks to his side again.

It is still hoped by those who have been profoundly shocked by Capdepont's outrageous behaviour that Rome may refuse to accept his nomination, but when Ternisien goes to the Vatican to put the case before the cardinal who is believed to be in charge of it, he is coldly received. The Superior of the Jesuit college at Lormières has sent a disingenuous account of the conflict: Ternisien and his friends are reprimanded for presumption in trying to influence the episcopal election; Rome believes it can make use of the strong man, Capdepont, and Evil is triumphant. Mgr Capdepont is soon further promoted to an archbishopric, and at the end of the book aspires to succeed Pius IX on the papal throne.

Fabre himself had been destined for the priesthood by the excellent uncle who took charge of him when his father, an architect, was ruined. He went to the Great Seminary at Montpellier, but felt that he had been commanded in a vision not to take holy orders. Perhaps he was also repelled by the two disadvantages of the priest's life, which

* Gosse, op. cit.

8

fully emerge in *Tigrane*. First, he is tied by the chain of ecclesiastical hierarchy, entirely dependent on the caprice of his bishop, and also bound by obedience to his more immediate superiors, who may order him to act against his conscience. Second, he is obliged to be loyal to his order, the clergy, and may not invoke the civil power however much he is in need of its help. Lavernède, Ternisien's ally, an excellent and courageous priest and most loyal to his bishop, is completely inhibited by these two obligations.

The obligation to celibacy does not distress any of the priests in this novel; Fabre believed that the unchaste priest was invented by Voltaire and not by the Devil. His priests may be full of ambition and hatred (like Capdepont), or cowardly and always ready to take the stronger side – he is sympathetic (for well he knows their difficulties) but never cynical or sentimental about them. They are never immoral, and even the worst of them, the intriguing Abbé Mical, is conscious of his divine vocation, and weeps for not having been more true to it. Neither George Eliot nor Trollope had any idea of vocation, or of the sacrament of holy order.

'Those who have lived among priests know that they are timid in general, and have little resistance to catastrophes that threaten their material position. Many are capable of dying for their God, few of meeting the common complications of life undisturbed' (pp. 17–18). This is illustrated even comically in the characters of the Archpriest Clamouse, now senile, and of the Abbé Turlot, the greasy professor of Holy Scripture, who alternately court Capdepont and Ternisien.

Moreover, as the Cardinal Maffeï explains to Ternisien, the Church and the government of the Church are two different things. The Church is 'divine, infallible, above human chances and changes'; but its government is obliged to fight against corruption and 'every form of culpable enterprise' – and it may have to lie. He shows Ternisien that it has little regard for justice, any more than any purely human institution. *Filii huius saeculi prudentiores sunt*; Ternisien, a child of light if ever there were one, goes away heart-broken back to his monastery at Tivoli. Victory is to the strong.

The topical interest of the novel is not so much insisted on that it has become dated, but at the time of its publication the Gallican and ultramontane disputes, which had come to their height in the first Vatican Council of 1869–70 and were halted by the proclamation of the dogma of papal infallibility, were still news. Capdepont, who had the Gallican views of the civil power (from whom he hoped for nomination to a bishopric), had translated Bossuet's *Déclaration* of the Assembly of French Clergy of 1682, which remained almost the charter of the Gallicans, though it had been condemned by Pope Alexander in 1689 and was later revoked by Louis XIV. After his nomination (when he was waiting for papal recognition) he began to express ultramontane views, and perhaps this won him the support of the Society of Jesus, which had always been ultramontane.

The religious orders, banished at the Revolution, were now returning to France, and many diocesan priests were jealous of the favours accorded to them by their bishops, Capdepont being among the first. He, however, when he had become Bishop of Lormières, placed the Great Seminary under the direction of the Jesuits, wishing to remain in the good graces of the Society.

Robert Liddell

THE ABBÉ TIGRANE

I

A PIOUS TOWN

Lormières is a small town of about fifteen thousand souls, hidden in a fold of the Corbières, mountains which connect the chain of the Cevennes with the Pyrenees. 'To see Lormières,' say the people of the place in their dialect, 'you must have your nose in the air.'

The town is divided into two quarters by a narrow watercourse, the Arbouse, whose source is in a picturesque wood of arbutus a few kilometres away. Below is the Quarter of the Paper-Mills, so called because of the numerous factories drawn up along the river; above is the Quarter of the Convents, which takes its name from the monasteries and churches that one sees on every hand. Here are the fine Gothic cathedral of St Irenaeus, the ancient Romanesque church of St Frument, the Barnabite cloister with its flamboyant rose window, and the heavy, massive buildings of the Great Seminary.

For that matter it was because of the multiplicity of religious establishments that the State Council justified the maintenance of an episcopate at Lormières in 1801, though it was not the chief town of a department – as there was a bishop's palace already built, why not send a bishop there? Church funds were so impoverished after the Revolution! For all these good reasons Monseigneur de la Guinaudie was appointed by Pope Pius VII at the consistory held in Rome on 3rd June 1802.

The streets of Lormières are narrow, winding and dark, and nearly all come out at the Arbouse, which is crossed by two bridges of ancient construction, somewhat squat perhaps, but embellished by parapets of free-stone which in the course of centuries have been polished from end to end by the touch of hands or by the mountain winds, and shine in the sun like mirrors.

13

In spite of these two ways of communication, which are more than sufficient, relations between the Quarter of the Convents and that of the Paper-Mills are rare. This is because of the radical difference between the manners and customs of the upper and lower town. While on the side of the factories a world of hands is at work, folding packets, nailing cases, loading carts, driving them to the station with the help of whips applied to the poor horses that pant and sweat and rear in anger, on the side of the cathedral the deepest silence reigns. The only sound heard there is that of church bells, or those of the communities which swarm in every direction: Dominicans, Jesuits, Marists, Carmelites, Visitation nuns, Sisters of the Holy Family, 'Reparatrices' of the heart of Mary – one gets lost among them.

Naturally such a wealth of priests and nuns could not fail to attract the noble houses of this privileged spot, and there are many nobles there.

Among other gentlemen who had long since been attracted to Lormières by its odour of sanctity we must mention the Vicomte de Castagnerte. It was there that this fiery champion of the Restoration, this agent so devoted and active (if anyone still recollects it) of the policy of the Prince de Polignac, retired after the July revolution. The King being dead, Monsieur de Castagnerte thought only of God, and left Paris to bury himself in the little town of the Corbières hills which Monseigneur d'Astros, the Archbishop of Toulouse, had indicated to him as a sort of antechamber to Paradise.

At Lormières the smallest feasts are observed; at Lormières the faithful – and there are only faithful there – dare pull rosaries out of their pockets in the open streets, and recite them piously; at Lormières one lives a life of austerity and retreat; at Lormières there is no theatre and the eyes of the penitent inhabitants have never been offended by a satanic encounter with a clown or a comedian. But like all souls who are half in Heaven, they make up for it when on the eve of Trinity Sunday or of Christmas his lordship the Bishop goes to the Great Seminary for the touching ceremony of ordination.

The Great Seminary of Lormières is a former convent of

Minims, with its back against the old wall that still encloses the upper town. The enormous wall is crowned by battlements, whose mossy stone has been crumbled by time; it runs the length of two courtyards where young clerics walk or play. These courtyards – one called that of the Subdeacons, the other that of the Tonsured – are planted with great elms which, in the season, give this austere almost savage retreat an incomparable coolness. All here breathes of antiquity, peace and contemplation.

In the early days of May 1866 the courtyard of the Subdeacons, usually quieter than that of the Tonsured, echoed with bursts of laughter interspersed by long and piercing shouts. Ball games had been organized, and everyone, with their cassocks picturesquely tucked up above their knees, did the best they could. Sometimes, among the brown or fair heads, a white head suddenly appeared, proving that more than one master was taking part in the fray.

Under the thick shade of the trees, not far from the battlefield, a priest was sitting on the stump of a column, a fragment of the Minims' cloister; he held a notebook in his hand. From time to time one of the players, his forehead streaming with sweat, ran up to this surly-looking priest and said: 'Six points to us, Mr Superior.'

Then the Abbé Rufin Capdepont, Vicar-General, titular Canon of the cathedral church of St Irenaeus, member of the diocesan council, professor of ecclesiastical history and Superior of the Great Seminary, took his pencil and wrote gravely.

Nevertheless, Abbé Capdepont cast from time to time an anxious glance towards the courtyard gate, as if he feared to be caught exercising functions so little in accord with sacerdotal dignity. One of his colleagues in the chapter might come in, or the Bishop himself, now recovered from a long illness . . . what would they say? What would they think?

For a moment, bothered by a physical need, the Superior left his notebook on the stone and stood up.

Abbé Capdepont was a tall, gaunt, thin man. He was about fifty years old. He had deep-set eyes; his nose, swollen like that of Pascal, was of monumental fullness; his mouth was severe, with thin, sinuous lips. His abundant hair, frizzy and going

15

grey – where the tonsure gave the effect of a moon seen through clouds – covered his finely sculptured head, and his complexion of yellowed ivory recalled the fine portraits of ascetics that we owe to the sombre genius of the Spanish masters.

'Mr Superior, two points for us, please,' stammered an abbé out of breath.

'Mark it yourself!' answered Capdepont, contemptuously showing the notebook.

He strode at a slow, stiff pace across the court, holding his head high and casting glances full of authority in all directions. Suddenly he trembled. The door of the chapel below the ramparts opened, and on the threshold appeared a little old man in a violet cassock, who supported himself on a stick with a gold knob.

'Monseigneur! Monseigneur!' cried the clerics, and their game stopped at once.

Abbé Rufin Capdepont advanced towards the Bishop without in any way abandoning his measured pace.

'You are slow in coming to ask us to accept your apology, Mr Superior,' said Monseigneur de Roquebrun, annoyed at the lack of haste made to welcome him.

'I had no idea that I owed your lordship an apology,' answered Capdepont in an arrogant tone.

'When an ecclesiastic of your rank shows so little compliance with his bishop's orders, he always owes him an apology. I have forbidden the ball game a hundred times. Why not leap-frog while you're about it?'

'I have frequently remarked to your lordship that in our seminaries in the South, from time immemorial these amusements . . .'

'No, sir! For nearly ten years you have been living in complete revolt against your bishop. Just now it was impossible for me to pray in the chapel because too much noise was being made everywhere. Is it these young people with their cassocks tucked up whom you mean to send shortly for ordination? Really, I am amazed at your young clerics' lack of modesty, and I blame myself for having left the direction of this establishment to you until now.'

16

'I am not anxious to keep it, and your lordship may confer it upon someone worthier.'

'Knowing you, I am aware that you mean to defy us to find a priest in the diocese capable of taking your place. What pride!'

'I am distressed that your lordship should give my thought an interpretation that could seem to lack justice and charity.'

This remark, insinuated in a tone of perfect propriety and with admirably simulated submission, was the last straw to Monseigneur de Roquebrun in his irritation. We should state, moreover, that if the lips of Abbé Capdepont had pronounced gentle and humble words, his eyes, lit by a sombre fire, had overwhelmed the Bishop with their terrible expression.

'Sir,' said the old man, whose face had suddenly gone purple, 'will you inform the directors of my Great Seminary that I await them in the conference chamber? I have a very serious communication to make to them. Little though you yourself care to know of our episcopal decisions, you will do well to accompany these gentlemen.'

Monseigneur de Roquebrun went back into the chapel, and with a brusque movement he pushed the door, which shut noisily.

II

MONSEIGNEUR DE ROQUEBRUN

The conference chamber was the former chapter house of the Minims. Narrow lancet windows obstructed by stone crossbars and by the leaves of the great elms, allowed only a pale, uncertain light to filter into this huge room, whose high vault with its sharp groins rested on three large pillars. The massive oak stalls, carved by the always rough but sometimes inspired chisel of an unknown artist, followed the line of the walls and joined in the chief panel opposite the entrance, the abbot's stall, a kind of throne to which one ascended by five steps. Above it, carved in the black wood, was the vigorous profile of St Francis de Paula, the founder of the community.

Monseigneur de Roquebrun, entering the conference chamber, made for the abbot's seat and sat down in it. The directors of the Seminary arrived slowly, one by one. The Bishop kept silence for a few minutes, perhaps to recollect the presence of God at this moment of great decision, perhaps merely to allow Abbé Rufin Capdepont who was late in coming, to arrive in time.

Finally, the Superior came in, his head thrust forward and his eyes on the floor – no doubt he feared he would be tempted to turn them a second time against his bishop. He walked to the last stall empty, and mechanically raised the wooden boss to lean upon. This movement, simple in itself, struck Monseigneur de Roquebrun. Being forewarned, he saw in it a clear intention to show lack of respect. 'Monsieur Capdepont,' he said, unable to control himself. 'This is my house, and I don't think I have yet authorized anyone to be seated.'

The Superior, with a bold movement like that of a horse hurt sharply by a spur, raised his head. 'Monseigneur,' he replied, 'the fourth Council of Carthage recommended the bishop never to allow one of his priests to stand while he himself was seated: *Episcopus, in quolibet loco sedens, non patiatur stare presbyterum . . .'*

'Sir, you are an excellent professor of ecclesiastical history, but I think it would be in good taste if you were to throw off your professional habits when talking to your bishop. Your knowledge of the Councils enchants me, but perhaps it would be becoming to add some *savoir-vivre* to all this balderdash.'

The last words were spoken with an exquisite impertinence, in which the gentleman appeared more than the bishop.

'Messieurs,' he added at once, to diminish the effect of his too sharp reply, 'I invite you to be seated.'

There was a long moment of silence.

'Gentlemen,' said Monseigneur de Roquebrun at last, in a quiet and grave tone, 'when ten years ago I came to take possession of the see of Lormières, my first care was in all ways to follow in the footsteps of my sainted predecessor. Nevertheless, after a few months, I understood that there were many reforms to be made in the diocese. I have attempted some. No one among you can have forgotten the complete reform of our liturgy. If I have not yet attempted the most important reform – I mean that of the Great Seminary – it is because almost insurmountable difficulties were in front of me. Before calling in priests from the religious orders to direct this establishment, was it not my duty to create an honourable situation for each of you? But where, in a diocese as poor as ours, could I find adequate compensation for clergy – whose ideas I might not altogether share, but whose intelligence and piety I have never ceased to recognize?. . . And why should I not confess that, despite my former conviction that the religious orders are better adapted than secular priests to form young levites, I always hoped to see things take a better turn, and not to be forced to make the changes which, with the deepest regret, I am carrying out today?'

The Bishop paused, and glanced round the room to see what was the effect of his short speech.

The effect was shattering. Apart from two or three heads held high against the storm, all were bowed in an attitude of consternation. Those who have lived among priests know that they are timid in general, and have little resistance to catastrophes that threaten their material position. Many are capable of dying for their God, few of meeting the common complications of life undisturbed.

One of the directors, the professor of moral theology, Abbé Mical, stood up – a little man, slim as a reed, with a mean face. 'Since your arrival, Monseigneur,' he said in a soft voice, 'You have filled Lormières and the diocese with the religious orders. May I venture to ask your lordship if it is the Jesuits, the Marists or the Dominicans who are to have the dangerous honour of taking our place?'

An ironical reproach sounded in each of these words.

'Are you so presumptuous as to oblige me to account to you for the acts of my administration, Monsieur Mical?' answered the Bishop haughtily.

'God forbid, Monseigneur! . . . But perhaps our services have deserved some regard. Perhaps we have the right to know to whom the fortunes of the students now torn from our care are to be entrusted, before we leave this house which has witnessed our sacrifices of many years.'

'Your right, sir, and your duty is to obey your bishop, alone charged by God and the Sovereign Pontiff with the direction of this diocese. You have no other right, do you understand?'

'I understand very well!' murmured the professor of moral theology, resuming his seat.

Abbé Turlot, professor of Holy Scripture, now rose in his turn: a fat, rotund man of an unhealthy pallor owing to excess of lymph in the blood. In a melancholy, almost tearful tone he ventured: 'Will my lord allow me to ask him a humble question?'

'Speak, sir.'

'If the changes that are to be made in the diocese are not already fixed . . .'

'Unfortunately they are already fixed.'

'What, it is all over?'

'Had we to consult you, Monsieur Turlot?'

'In this case, would your lordship be so very kind as to let me know to what post you assign me?'

Monseigneur de Roquebrun took up his gold-rimmed lorgnette and cast his eyes over a large sheet of paper which he had held spread out in front of him since his entry into the council chamber.

'Monsieur Turlot, on the day following the ordination, which I have fixed for the twenty-sixth of this month, eve of the Most Holy Trinity, you will go to take possession of the chaplaincy of the prisons, vacant because of the death of Abbé Vidal.'

'I, a prison chaplain, I!' stammered the poor professor of Holy Scripture, terrified, and with eyes full of tears. 'But Lord Jesus! Where shall I find the courage if I have to accompany a condemned criminal to the scaffold?'

'You will ask God to grant it to you.'

'Oh, Monseigneur, I swear I shan't be able. . . .'

Without further attention to the laments of Monsieur Turlot, the Bishop continued: 'After agreement with his excellency the Minister of Justice and Ecclesiastical Affairs, we have appointed Abbé Mical as rural dean of Bastide-sur-Mont, a canton of the third class.'

The malicious professor of moral theology did not turn a hair; he went on playing with the tassels of his rich silk girdle, a habitual gesture.

'Monsieur Lavernède,' continued Monseigneur de Roque-brun, 'we appoint you chaplain to the orphanage founded by us at Bastide-sur-Mont. A new post.'

'Poor mother!' murmured Lavernède in a strangled voice.

The Bishop was moved, and looked at him. 'Are you ill, sir?' he asked with a delicate tone of sympathy.

Abbé Lavernède, professor of sacred rhetoric, the most distinguished of the directors of the Seminary after Abbé Capdepont, was horribly pale. 'It's nothing, Monseigneur,' he murmured. 'My mother. . . .'

He was unable to finish his phrase.

'Your mother?' insisted Monseigneur de Roquebrun anxiously.

'She's eighty-two and an invalid. She won't be able to endure the journey from Lormières to Bastide-sur-Mont. . . . But how can I leave her? She has no one but me. . . . Never mind!' he added in a firmer tone. 'I'm a priest, and it isn't I who will ever utter the terrible word of Scripture, *Non serviam*, "I won't obey!" I'm in the hands of God and of my bishop.'

'Your words do you honour, sir,' said Monseigneur de Roquebrun, his little eyes suddenly wet with emotion. 'I'm sorry my private secretary, who respects you and is attached to you, did not tell me what touching duties tie you to Lormières.'

'Your secretary is a foreigner, and for this reason he ought not to be allowed to interest himself in the affairs of the diocesan clergy,' intercepted Abbé Rufin Capdepont, suddenly abandoning his impassibility.

The Bishop, amazed at this audacity, looked at the Superior of the Great Seminary almost with stupefaction. Then with an air of crushing mockery he said: 'Perhaps, with your almost untrained character, sir, you don't know that you have been impertinent. If you don't know that, I hasten to tell you.'

Abbé Capdemont bit his lips and remained silent.

'Monsieur Lavernède,' went on Monseigneur de Roquebrun, 'we take into consideration the family duties that keep you in our episcopal city, and as an act of grace authorize an exchange between Monsieur Turlot and yourself. Monsieur Turlot will go to Bastide-sur-Mont and you will take the chaplaincy of the prisons which alarms him.'

Although the Bishop had taken up the interruption of Abbé Capdepont severely, he had been deeply hurt by the rude interference of the one with whom he had already had too many disputes over matters outside that person's competence. Moreover, had he not attacked his private secretary, his friend, his child, Abbé Ternisien, a model priest, a saint? He could hardly pass over such an insult without disloyalty to friendship, even to God!

Monseigneur de Roquebrun, a natural fighter, too irritable for a ministry of peace and conciliation, still felt his nerves tingling. He could no longer contain himself and, looking at the Superior of the Great Seminary from head to foot, he said: 'I fancy, sir, that just now you allowed yourself to speak of Abbé Ternisien. Will you kindly explain yourself?'

'I only observed to your lordship', said Abbé Capdepont – whose sleeve Abbé Mical had furtively plucked, no doubt to persuade him to be calm – 'that Monsieur Ternisien, in declining to interfere in Monsieur Lavernède's affairs, had shown perfect understanding of his limited position as a foreigner.'

'So it is I who have not understood my position as bishop

when I brought Monsieur Ternisien into the diocese?'

'Perhaps.'

'Frankly I am delighted to learn that it is myself alone whom you are pleased to honour with your attacks. Well, what have you to reproach me with?'

'What have I to reproach you with?' cried Abbé Capdepont in a strident tone, stepping forward from his stall. 'I reproach you for your passion for reform, for not allowing us to keep our saints' days, for having practically abolished the *Proper** of the diocese of Lormières, one of the most ancient and glorious in the martyrology of the Church of France. I reproach you for a finical, vexatious administration, above all disastrous for the poor clergy whom you move about for the most futile reasons – and for a haughtiness of speech and attitude which may not seem out of place in the caste to which you are so proud of belonging, but has always been so in the Church, where the Divine Master has proclaimed the equality of everyone. Only the other day did you not say to the priest in charge of Moutiers when he humbly asked if you would leave him for a long time in his new parish, *Quamdiu nobis placuerit* – "As long as it pleases us." Finally, I reproach you for giving up the diocese as a prey to the regular clergy. Is there in the department a town, a village, where the parochial clergy have not had to struggle against the encroachment of the religious corporations? Everywhere, even in the remotest corner of our mountains, the Marists, the Fathers of Hope, the Passionists build chapels, open oratories and starve your priests, who are powerless against this invasion. Oh, I know in Rome they are pleased with your compliance, and that in return for such generous sacrifices you have lately received the right to wear the *cappa magna* and the cross of Gregory the Great. These honours had their price, but your clergy find them bought too dear . . .'

'Take care, sir,' interrupted the Bishop, with an indulgent mockery designed to exasperate Monsieur Capdepont. 'Between you and me, I think you're going rather too far. Knowing you of old, I care nothing for your outbursts against

---

* That part of the office books containing feasts peculiar to the diocese.

23

me – I'm used to them. But if you dare to attack the decisions of the Sovereign Pontiff . . .'

'The gift of a decoration or a silk vestment is certainly not a dogmatic decision, and what I've said about sacerdotal vanities can't be considered as an attack on the Holy Father, whom I respect and honour.'

'Ah, moderation at last. I congratulate you. Go on.'

The terrible Superior was disconcerted by the Bishop's ironical invitation. He stood for a moment in the middle of the conference chamber without noticing that he had moved there, and he looked vacantly in front of him. He wiped his forehead, which was sparkling with drops of sweat. His extreme anger made it impossible for him to resume the thread of his ideas – he abandoned all the invective he still had to hurl in the face of Monseigneur de Roquebrun, and asked Abbé Mical's question again as a way of making a fairly honourable retreat.

'May I ask in my turn, Monseigneur, if it is the Marists or the Dominicans or the Lazarites who are to take possession of this establishment after ourselves?'

'You are concerned about this?'

'It would be strange not to be, when we are obliged to bequeath to the newcomers the most precious heritage – that of picked intelligences and of simple, pious hearts.'

'Be satisfied: they are the Fathers of Catholic Instruction of the diocese of Arras.'

'The Fathers of Catholic Instruction!' cried Abbé Capdepont, again flying into a passion. 'But that body is completely unknown! It is for these gentlemen that you are turning us out?'

'This is too much!' retorted Monseigneur de Roquebrun, tired, and determined to make an end of it. 'I am your bishop, sir,' he added, with great dignity. 'And I summon you from the twenty-seventh of this month of May to go and occupy your stall as titular Canon of the chapter of St Irenaeus, if you don't want to be turned away from there as from here.'

'You are the master!' said Abbé Capdepont in a deep voice, slowly regaining his place.

The old Bishop stood up, with a sudden movement of his knees. Indignation had roused him. 'Monsieur L'Abbé,' he said, 'you have uttered words full of hatred and perhaps the desire of revenge. I have not forgotten, sir, that when by the free choice of the Sovereign Pontiff I was elected Bishop of Lormières, you were a candidate for the throne which I occupy. You had no need to remind me of this by your outbursts. Thanks to your numerous protectors in Paris – I say nothing of Rome – it is possible that you may one day be raised to the episcopate. Meanwhile you will obey the first authority in this diocese, or that authority will break you.'

In spite of Abbé Mical, who tried to restrain him, Abbé Capdepont, whose blood was now boiling, bowed and went out.

Abbé Lavernède rose. 'Monseigneur,' he said, 'I am sorry that my name served as a pretext for a deplorable scene. I beg you to believe that I had in no way asked the Superior of the Great Seminary to defend my interests to your lordship. For many years there have been no ties between Abbé Capdepont and me, save the inevitable ties of the priesthood.'

'Gentlemen,' said the Bishop, recovering some of his calm, 'I shall provide later on for those of you for whom I have not yet assigned a post.'

And after shaking hands with Abbé Lavernède, an honour of which he was sparing, he took his hat and stick and left the Great Seminary without looking behind him.

III

RUFIN CAPDEPONT

Monseigneur de Roquebrun was not a man to deceive himself; the blow he had just struck was terrible, and the secret war declared against him by his clergy, worked on by Abbé Capdepont, could not fail to break out openly.

Despite these acute worries, the little old man went out alone through the winding streets of the Quarter of the Convents, tapping his stick on the pebbled street and stopping, as he had the gentle habit of doing, at the doors of houses to bless and caress the children. As the weather was fine and his head, heated by the stormy meeting at the Great Seminary, needed fresh air, he went as far as the Quarter of the Paper-Mills.

Monseigneur de Roquebrun liked the Quarter of the Paper-Mills and visited it from time to time, going into factories, where he was received with marks of respectful affection, slipping into the humblest households and giving alms. 'Monseigneur, come up to my house! Come up to my house!' called the women who saw him in the street.

He, simple as an apostle, in spite of the pride with which Abbé Capdepont reproached him, climbed up rickety stairs, took a rough straw chair and sat down. Then the same lamentations rained on him: the price of bread had gone up; the man was ill . . . the little ones needed clothes . . . and the good Bishop gave, gave and gave.

Everyone knew that Monseigneur de Roquebrun had been rich when he came into the diocese and was poor today. Had he not lately sold his carriage and horses to help a poor industrialist to replace the walls of his factory, carried off by a sudden flooding of the Arbouse? So now he went about on foot, finding an unspeakable pleasure in his new condition. 'I see my poor from near at hand,' he said to Abbé Ternisien, who was well off and wanted to make a present of a new equipage to

26

this old man, whom he loved and who, he was afraid, would tire himself too much.

If the Bishop of Lormières had been able to control a hot-blooded petulance, which sometimes forced him into violent speech, we cannot doubt that he would have enjoyed the popular sanctity of a Cheverus or a Miollis. In fact, in charity and every sort of beneficence his life was in no way behind that of those noble and devoted examples of the French episcopate. Moreover, let us hasten to say that the faults of Monseigneur de Roquebrun, in particular concerning his visit to the Great Seminary, were more in appearance than reality. Ever since his arrival at Lormières he had paid every delicate attention possible to Abbé Rufin Capdepont with the clear intention to win him to himself. But nothing could gain the sympathy of this hard, imperious character. It was in vain that the Bishop, who had soon discovered the ambitions of the Superior of the Great Seminary, obtained for him the cross of the Legion of Honour from the Government; and in vain he later appointed him titular Canon of St Irenaeus, to add to his income. Capdepont kept within the limits of formal thanks, and never uttered a word to give hope that his heart had been touched. Fundamentally, the Superior did not forgive Monseigneur de Roquebrun for occupying a see on which he had had an eye, and which he pretended had been promised to him. He would never forgive him this. To this sullen, unconquerable man the actual Bishop of Lormières was a usurper, and nothing more.

But let us pause for a moment to consider this singular and most individual personage.

The Abbé Rufin Capdepont was born about 1815 at the very edge of the diocese, on the Spanish frontier in the little village of Harros. He did not come to Lormières till he was twenty years old, to enter the Great Seminary. His classical studies had been scamped in his native hamlet under an old priest who was more interested in setting nets for trout in the mountain streams than in cultivating the intelligence of the young Rufin. Luckily the soil was good and, whatever negligence went to the sowing, the few grains of seed that fell from time to time into the furrows put forth ears so rapidly that the pupil himself asked for new masters and wished to leave the district.

Capdepont's first days at the Seminary, which he entered with a scholarship from the diocese, were not without suffering and bitterness. Young people have the faults of their age even under the strictest discipline: they are mocking, teasing, aggressive. Capdepont, whose features were rubbed by the passage of time to blend in harmony, and whose face had finally taken on a character of cold rigidity, which was not without nobility and distinction, had at twenty an angular, pale face with yellowish eyes that looked as if their holes had been made with gimlets, and a long, broad nose with a very evident scar at the end, and tousled hair as prickly as a holly bush. 'What a mug! What a mug!' cried his fellow students, romping round him.

Youth has to be lived through in a seminary as much as elsewhere. He ought to have laughed. But no, his fists were clenched. He would gladly have pounced on his enemies.

One day a tonsured clerk, Mical, malicious as a monkey, had laughed at the untidy, tasteless way in which the native of Harros put his clerical bands round his long neck, like that of a stork. Capdepont rushed at him with uplifted arm; then, controlling his savage temper, he walked away to an isolated corner and shed the tears of rage that filled his eyes.

An unpleasant characteristic of southern people is their passion for giving nicknames. What was to be that of the new seminarist? The young heads went to work.

One morning in the Church history lesson the professor asked young Rufin: 'Can you tell me the name of one of the kings who joined with Cyrus in the sack of Babylon?'

'Tigranes, King of Armenia,' replied Capdepont.

All his fellow students looked at him in amazement. The word for which they had been searching had been found. 'Tigrane! Tigrane!' they cried at him on every side when it was recreation time.

At first the vigorous peasant of Harros could not control himself, and catching hold of Abbé Lavernède, the first of his comrades who fell under his hand, he seized him by the wrist and threw him brutally to the ground.

'Ah, tiger . . . you're a tiger!' groaned poor Lavernède, whose knee had been grazed and had left more than one drop of blood on the pebbles of the court.

28

But it was no use Capdepont using violence; his instincts had been well guessed, and ever afterwards he was called only **Abbé Tigrane.**

What was he to do? How to put a truce to persecutions that had become intolerable? His pride showed Capdepont only one way to obtain his important result; he must raise himself above all the others by his conduct and industry. On the day when he was the first pupil in the class and the directors publicly attested his good behaviour, who would dare to attack him?

All went as he wished. Eight months after he had entered the Great Seminary Abbé Rufin Capdepont had conquered all his masters by his continued successes and had reduced to silence his fellow pupils, all astonished and abashed at having so misjudged him.

In the vacations, when everyone went happily to his family, our young cleric, in all the fervour of his studies, asked and obtained permission not to leave the Great Seminary. In fact, what was he to do in his mountains? To see his mother again? But he knew his mother was well. To see the old priest, his first master? But what intellectual profit could he derive from that visit? If only he were to find at Harros the inexhaustible library that he could consult here at any minute! He remained, passing his days in reading or meditation, his evenings in conversation, becoming more and more intimate with the directors.

Oh, what discussions, debates, dissertations in the great empty courts of the Subdeacons and of the Tonsured, by the light of the stars! In these arguments between professors in which the young abbé did not yet dare place a word his mind, always awake, became singularly sharpened for scholastic dispute. When would he be able to speak with the same facility and brilliance as his masters?

After the most heated discussions about dogma, moral philosophy, Church history, the professors who had most vigorously disputed were long asleep when he, wanting to form an opinion on the case at issue, crept stealthily down to the library, looked up the texts that had been cited, and often passed the greater part of the night at his task.

Abbé Rufin Capdepont received the minor orders, and the subdeaconate a year later. It was about this time that, finding himself irrevocably committed to a clerical life, he began to consider how to direct his powers to studies that might most usefully serve his career. Casuistry was certainly not his bent. His fiery, passionate nature needed to contend with men rather than with trifling subtleties, and he thought history was the real field to satisfy his intellect. And what history is more attractive, more grandiose than that of the Church, which through the centuries is an epitome of the history of the world? Such fascination! The popes establishing the unity of doctrine; the popes, the real kings of the universe, effecting the investiture of kingdoms; the popes in a manner moulding Europe, drawing all monarchies on earth to the divine type of the government of the Church. And what a vision! Sixtus V, a simple swineherd, had one day been able to rise to the papal throne, the highest and the most brilliant of all! . . .

Capdepont, infatuated by the splendour of his vision, remembered that, innocent of this, he had several times in his childhood driven young boars to pick up acorns in the oak forests above Harros. Moreover, had not his patron, Tyrannius Rufinus, clearly shown him the way to follow – had he not translated into Latin the fourth-century *Ecclesiastical History* of Eusebius of Caesarea?

At twenty-five years of age Abbé Capdepont was ordained priest and attached as curate to the parish of St Frument at Lormières. The Bishop, aware of his academic success, did not wish to place so distinguished a subject at a distance from himself.

However, in spite of further testimonies of good will received from Monseigneur Grandin, the fourth successor of Monseigneur de la Guinaudie, Capdepont felt overcome by an unconquerable boredom after only two years as an assistant priest, first at St Frument and then at St Irenaeus. Administering the sacraments to the sick, burying the dead, hearing the confessions of incorrigible, pious women – all these tasks, carried out without a murmur, at bottom distracted him terribly. What would these duties lead to, however punctually performed? Perhaps after twenty years he would be appointed rural dean of some poor district in the mountains. Was it for this that he had grown pale over his books, that he still slaved at his studies and was preparing, for a celebrated Paris publisher, a new translation of the works of St Thomas Aquinas, with notes? He had, cost what it might, to turn back to a life engrossed by these wretched duties, drowned (so to speak) in professional commonplaces for which so many others were more fit than he.

Alas, how could he shake off his yoke, how conquer his liberty?

He had a plan.

Rufin Capdepont, who was from time to time invited with the higher clergy of the diocese to the salons of the bishop's palace where once a week Monseigneur Grandin received the aristocracy of Lormières led by the Vicomte de Castagnerte, had there made the acquaintance of the Baron Thévenot, formerly a local mill-owner. Thévenot had made money in the manufacture of paper and since 1830 replaced Monsieur de Castagnerte in Parliament; it was to his obedience to the Ministry as much as his perpetual self-effacement that he owed the title of baron. Nevertheless, he was an agreeable man, well read, and well informed on financial and industrial questions, and capable of being useful in committee.

About 1832 Thévenot had married, in Paris, a demoiselle Baladier, fresh, pretty, and a little frivolous, so the noble tongues of the Quarter of the Convents said. After the proper time she presented her husband with a fat pink and white boy, a magnificent German doll.

What was to be done with the new arrival? What education would fit the future baron? It was not the child's father who put this question but Capdepont, the first time he met the member for Lormières accompanied by his inevitable Edmond. What an achievement: to get permission to leave the diocese and go with Baron Thévenot to Paris as his son's tutor . . . to Paris!

No obstacle can thwart people of the vigorous stamp of our rough mountaineer of Harros. Lurking behind the Baronne Thévenot, who had been persuaded by his eloquence, Abbé Capdepont overcame the opposition of the Bishop, who obstinately wished to keep him at hand; he overcame the resistance of the deputy who had resolved to make Edmond

31

follow the liberal course at the Lycée St Louis, and finally, at the beginning of the season, he left Lormières, solidly fixed in the position he had desired.

This was in the first days of 1843.

The Thévenot household had found its master. There are characters whom fate cannot keep down in inferior positions: they break the narrow frameworks meant to enclose them, and spread out over all that surrounds them. At first Capdepont seemed to confine himself strictly to his duties as a tutor; but after three months he was absent for a few days on a visit to a friend of his at St Germain, a Monsieur Jérôme Bonnardot, distant cousin of the Minister of Ecclesiastical Affairs. At once a great vacuum was felt in the rue de Lille, in the house of the member for Lormières. Not only had Edmond nothing to do, and kept asking for his tutor; not only was the Baronne, who could not buy a little bit of lace without consulting the Abbé, and often bothered him, now crying for his return; but the Baron accustomed to hear the advice, perhaps the orders of Capdepont on returning from the House, declared he could not live without him, and was simple enough to let him know it.

The Abbé came back in triumph to the rue de Lille. Energetically he seized again the threads of the little government of the Thévenot house, which he patiently unravelled, and made to serve his ambition. At thirty he could hardly expect to be made a bishop; but the episcopate had become his incessant, overmastering dream. He must work, work without respite to make smooth the paths that inevitably led there. To attain so lofty an object he must use all the resources he had in hand: Monsieur Thévenot's wealth, his large acquaintance and his luxurious style of living; above all he must turn to account the charming, witty frivolity of the Baronne, who was well known in the official world, and well able, if she set her mind to it, to bewitch the Minister of Ecclesiastical Affairs and get out of him a definite promise when the moment came.

If, as St Clement of Alexandria has written, 'the habit of chastity hardens the heart', one may say that the habit of ambition withers it. We shall have been quite unsuccessful in describing the character of Rufin Capdepont if the reader has had the smallest suspicions about his relations with Madame Thévenot. This priest, glum in face and brief in speech and imperious in gesture, was quite out of his element in the world of gallantry. He had absolutely nothing in common with the scented, roguish libertine abbés of the last century.

Moreover, why not declare that Capdepont had a high sense of duty, that he was pious, faithful in all religious practices, and capable of the strictest probity? Born in the lowest rank of society and tormented – atrocious agony – by a superior talent, he aspired to rise above the mire of his birth and encroach on the episcopate; but his clerical character was one of integrity, and no consideration could have made him infringe it. He respected the Baronne Thévenot, he honoured her; but this woman could contribute to the success of his enterprise and, carried away by the violence of his fixed idea, he employed her blindly. The strength of his passion prevented him from feeling that this was not very delicate, and made it incomprehensibly simple. It was not a question of audacity on his part, or corruption, so much as naïveté.

Formerly Baron Thévenot had one reception a month; now Capdepont made him give a dinner every week, and each Tuesday the doors of the house in the rue de Lille were open to guests.

It was a great surprise to the peers and deputies and high officials who regularly came to the house to see the ecclesiastical element stealthily filter in. At first one saw only one pair of clerical bands at table, the great silk bands of Abbé Capdepont – then one saw two, three, four pairs. Finally, one evening when the conversation was becoming heated between some hardened Voltaireans and Edmond's haughty tutor, who tried to be all things to all men, the usher suddenly announced: 'Monseigneur, the Archbishop of Paris'.

'Does Thévenot go to confession?' sniggered some bald-headed men, who went away at once.

The member for Lormières, confused and sheepish, was perhaps going to lay the blame on Capdepont and reproach him for compromising him, when he felt someone seize his hand.

'Very good, Baron,' said the malicious Marquis de Boissy. 'You welcome the clergy when they're in such disfavour at the

Château; that's courage.' Then, turning to a pretty woman, 'Goodbye, dear friend,' he said. 'I'll come back when I wish to be converted.' And in his turn he slipped away.

On 21st December 1847 Baron Thévenot, who had never mounted the rostrum, suddenly did so. As might be guessed, there was general amazement.

'Where are you going like that, my lad?' asked President Dupin, who had known him since 1830 and had even appeared at some of the Tuesdays.

Unmoved, the deputy for Lormières began a long discourse on ecclesiastical pensions.

'Enough, enough!' cried the House.

Thévenot went on. Then, having pronounced the last phrase of his discourse, which was a text taken from St Augustine, he came down proudly.

'It's a real *capucinade*!'* said Marshal Soult.

'I beg your pardon, you're not there,' retorted the elder Dupin. 'It's a *cap . . . depontade.*'

There was laughter, and it was quoted in the papers for a week.

However, Abbé Capdepont was drawing near to his objective. On 31st December, some days after the endless harangue he had imposed upon the obedient Thévenot, he learned from Monsieur Jérôme Bonnardot, who had heard it from the Ministry of Ecclesiastical Affairs, that his name had been placed on the list of candidates for the episcopate.

What joy!

Unfortunately there was talk of reformist banquets, and the political horizon was growing more and more gloomy.

The February revolution broke out.

There was great terror in the house in the rue de Lille. Baron Thévenot, to whom fear gave courage, had his trunks packed in haste despite protests from his wife, and they left for Lormières.

Rufin Capdepont was grave: the events that surprised him when he was in full flight towards his objective, and threatened to break his wings, threw him into dismay. But he came to after his stupefactions, and they had spent hardly a fortnight in the

---

* *Capucinade:* a long, boring sermon.

South before he was quite his own man again, with the same ambition and the same energy to realize it.

At this time of confusion there was one rumour that dominated the department, that of the election of a Constituent Assembly. Capdepont encouraged the poor Baron, still bruised by his fall, and made him put himself forward as a duty. Monseigneur Grandin would address a circular to the priests of his diocese in support of his candidature, and his success was certain.

Alas, what occurred was just the opposite of the prediction of the indefatigable abbé: the electors thought Monsieur Thévenot too much involved with the Catholic party and inflicted on him the most mortifying check. When he needed at least forty thousand votes, he received barely three thousand, five hundred.

Rufin Capdepont thought seriously. Evidently the vessel on which he had embarked with all he had was letting in water everywhere; he would never arrive at the episcopate. His interests – perhaps those of Heaven also – required him to leave the Thévenot family before complete shipwreck. Besides, who knew if it would not be extremely clever, when the republicans reproached the former deputy of Lormières for putting his son into the hands of a priest, to put Edmond into a lycée? This man, so clever and persistent in his designs, persuaded Thévenot whenever he wished. The Baron was broken by his latest setback in the elections, and by the discovery of the hole made in his fortune by the extravagances of Paris; and Edmond's departure for the lycée of Toulouse was decided at once.

The day after his pupil's departure Abbé Capdepont left the fine Thévenot house by the Arbouse, not far from the Paper-Mills, and shut himself up in the Great Seminary where, as a special favour, Monseigneur Grandin had allowed him to make a retreat for a few days. This priest, whose life till now had been a long fever, had need to collect himself. It was the most solemn moment of his life; his future depended on the decision he would have to take.

Meeting his former fellow student, Abbé Mical, who held the chair of moral theology at the Great Seminary, he revealed his most secret plans to him, and asked his advice at this hour of

35

extreme anguish. For his own part he inclined to return at once to Paris. He would take up his connections again, would see Monsieur Jérôme Bonnardot, who was ever ready to serve him, and some former peers become representatives of the people; then he would take his degrees at the faculty of theology and acquire the title of professor. Had not the Sorbonne been a nursery for bishops under all governments?

The ironic Mical shook his head incredulously, and pressed his friend not to leave Lormières.

'What am I to do here?' asked Capdepont.

'Here! What you like. You can be Superior of the Great Seminary and at the same time professor of ecclesiastical history, if you want.'

'It seems to me that both these posts are occupied.'

'Yes, but old Gaudron, crippled with illness, is continually asking to be replaced.'

'And my bishopric?'

'Why, of course, you'll be Bishop of Lormières.'

'You really have a way of unpeopling the diocese . . .'

'Of Monseigneur Grandin? . . . My dear, he has tubercular laryngitis. My brother Dr Mical told me that. You can suffer for a long time with this illness, but in the end it carries you off. You could have a quiet talk with my brother . . .'

'I'll stay,' said Capdepont, squeezing his friend's hand. 'I'll stay.'

As soon as he was Superior of the Great Seminary, Rufin Capdepont was in the diocese of Lormières what he had been in the Thévenot family; he had to be master in everything. Dominating the Bishop, who had shut himself up in his palace and never went out any more, he busied himself with the smallest details of administration, and missed no opportunity of making felt his authority as Vicar-General, for he had forced this title from the weak Monseigneur Grandin. He thought it would help his further plans if he knew all the clergy, and urged the sick prelate to stay snugly at home, getting from Paris an acquaintance of his own, a Bishop of Jericho *in partibus* with whom by short stages he went all round the diocese to administer confirmation, from the chief town of the department to the most wretched hamlet.

'Gentlemen,' said Monseigneur de Jericho, introducing Capdepont, 'here's your future bishop.'

At last, in July 1855, Monseigneur Grandin decided to die.

Rufin Capdepont rushed to Paris, and brought all his world to white heat. He saw the Archbishop, the Minister, several senators, a dozen deputies. He even found the means to be presented to the Empress, who graciously received him.

But no news came to the Hôtel du Bon La Fontaine in the rue Grenelle, where he was staying.

At last Monsieur Jérôme Bonnardot turned up one evening.

'Well?' asked Capdepont, devoured by violent anxiety.

'My dear friend,' answered Bonnardot, who still kept up relations with the Ministry of Ecclesiastical Affairs, despite the fall of his cousin, a minister of Louis-Philippe's. 'General Comte de Roquebrun, a senator, has gone to Compiègne, and has carried off the nomination of his brother, the Abbé Armand de Roquebrun, Canon of Arras.'

Capdepont was overwhelmed, and struck dumb.

'Moreover, it seems that Abbé de Roquebrun was not a new candidate. As early as 1843 the Cardinal de la Tour d'Auvergne had pointed him out to the King, and the pious Queen Marie-Amélie had warmly recommended him. . . . Courage, then. Go back to Lormières – the honourable position you hold there will naturally. . . . Besides, you're still young . . .'

'Young! I'm forty-one, sir.'

'Well, Monseigneur de Roquebrun is sixty.'

'Monseigneur de Roquebrun, you say!' cried Capdepont in a grim temper. 'Don't speak to me of that man, I hate him!'

IV

DIOCESAN ADMINISTRATION

When he found that all his kind attentions directed to Abbé Capdepont were a pure loss, Monseigneur de Roquebrun felt deeply distressed. Evidently it was an irreconcilable enemy who had risen against him, and it was beneath his dignity to make any further advances. What particularly grieved him was to see his Seminary in the hands of a man whose doctrine, in his own view, was far from orthodox.

Rufin Capdepont, in fact, had followed the movement which in the first years of the Empire led a large part of the clergy into Gallican ideas. Perhaps these priests, stubborn champions of the liberties of the Church of France that the First Consul had maintained in the celebrated articles of the Concordat, were neither the most honest nor the purest; but no doubt they were the most active, and Capdepont could not fail to go along with them.

Monseigneur de Roquebrun was furious, disgusted that the moment chosen for attacking his authority should be when the Sovereign Pontiff was overwhelmed by public events. 'The meanness of it, the meanness of it!' he said again and again to his secretary, Ternisien.

The Bishop of Lormières was extremely unhappy. But how could he get rid of Abbé Capdepont, whom he himself had so much praised at the beginning of his episcopate both in Rome and Paris, because he had been amazed at the learning of the Superior of the Great Seminary and edified by his austere piety? Ah, why had his heart once again outstripped his intelligence?

Certainly the old man hated to be obliged to reverse his opinion. If he withdrew Capdepont from the Great Seminary to give him an inferior post, he risked the fierce Canon refusing him face to face, and going straight to Paris – and then what might not happen? Who knew if this man, distracted by hatred, would not let loose all his supporters against his enemy? Whom could he fail to convince, gifted as he was with immense ability, and with a fiery and seductive eloquence?

Certainly had only he himself been in question, Monseigneur de Roquebrun felt he was quite capable of taking on the struggle. But why distress the Holy Father, already so unhappy, by provoking a new scandal in the Church? The Bishop of Lormières remembered how the Bishop of Pamiers had been almost dragged out of his see by the police as a result of the intrigues of his clergy, and resigned himself to putting up with Capdepont as a punishment for his sins.

However, false situations give rise only to false security, and in spite of Monseigneur de Roquebrun's firm resolve to avoid the Superior of the Great Seminary, the Bishop and the Canon soon met again face to face. The two men seemed to need to fall foul of each other.

It must, moreover, be said that Rufin Capdepont had a passion for running into his enemy. The Bishop could not appear at the most insignificant ceremony in the chapel of the Dominicans or the Lazarites but Capdepont, who detested the regulars and made no secret of it, was there, tormenting him with his look of hatred and inviting him by every provocative attitude to give battle without further challenge. Tigrane was ever on the watch, ready to pounce on his prey.

This fever of persecution in the rough mountaineer of Harros was due to the long martyrdom of his ambition. 'To be good in suffering, one must be more than a man,' wrote Lammenais. In vain, for ten years, every time a bishopric fell vacant, had Capdepont made the journey to Paris; in vain, so that no doubt might arise about his opinions concerning civil power, had he re-edited Bossuet's famous *Déclaration* to the Assembly of the Clergy in 1682 with a very explicit preface; in vain had he taken his head to the Tuileries to have the big Gallican bump that had grown on his forehead felt by a celebrated professor of the Sorbonne, charged specially with a course of clerical phrenology. The bishoprics were filled, and he was left forgotten at Lormières. Did they mean never to come to him? Finally, he grew tired of waiting.

In his despair, Rufin Capdepont's temper knew no bounds;

he laid the blame on everyone round him. He ceaselessly tormented Abbé Mical and hit him, one day striking a blow with his fist that left him unconscious for a quarter of an hour. Above all he blamed Monseigneur de Roquebrun, who had stolen what was his: the mitre, the crosier and the ring. Had not the Empress herself told him at Compiègne in November 1855, 'It will be you!'

Laymen cannot understand what it is for a priest to become a bishop. Yesterday you were a simple soldier in an army of eighty thousand men – there are about eighty thousand clerics in France. Today, all of a sudden, you are a general; the change is as abrupt as that. The curate, the rural dean, the canon, the vicar-general all have the same restricted canonical rights; only the bishop possesses priesthood in plenitude. And then, what a different position in the world! You are a prince of the Holy Roman Church; you are called 'My lord'; the Pope calls you simply 'venerable brother'. He cannot do without you if he wants to publish a decision relative to dogma or discipline; you go to Rome *ad limina apostolorum*, as they say, and you are received at the Vatican with the distinction paid to sovereigns. Who knows if, now you have the mitre of a bishop, you may not later get the hat of a cardinal? Who knows if, in the course of the revolutions not uncommon in our times, you may not one day wear the tiara? Was not Urban IV the son of a cobbler of Troyes? Was not John XXII born at Cahors?

Rufin Capdepont's passionate imagination had dwelt lovingly on these mad dreams. How often in the silence of the Minims' cloister had this man, born to command, reprimanded *his* priests and operated the most radical reforms in an imaginary diocese. And after all those promises, people broke their word to him. Were all the hopes cherished in his long life of torment to come pitifully to grief? Did they not consider in Paris that he was getting on for fifty? Ah, when they put a crosier in his hand, they would see things! To pay the Government out for the intolerable delay he felt capable of anything, even of turning to Rome and becoming as ultramontane as Monseigneur de Roquebrun.

Nevertheless, despite the irritating insistence of the Superior of the Great Seminary to throw himself in his way, the Bishop of Lormières had avoided exchanging a word with him. He pretended not to see Capdepont, and walked by with dignity. But one could guess from his involuntary movements and an expression of vexation that the old man was near the end of his tether and that Abbé Ternisien, a lover of concord and of peace at any price, would not long be able to hold him back.

Finally, the storm that had been brewing for years broke out terrifically at a session of the diocesan court.

Though he was a member of that tribunal, Capdepont, kept in the Great Seminary by his duties as Superior, and as professor of ecclesiastical history, had never appeared there until he suddenly decided to occupy his seat on 5th August 1865 when an insignificant case came up, of a wretched curate accused by the chief of the department of getting on badly with his mayor.

'Monsieur Capdepont,' said the Bishop, who was naturally president of the court, 'you have come too late. The case has been heard and decided.'

'I should all the same have something to say.'

'It is very conscientious of you, sir, but the decisions have been recorded, and your eloquence cannot help your client.'

'I have not been able to speak. My right to do so therefore remains unqualified.'

The Bishop looked as if he were going to rise.

'I protest against the decision given!' cried Capdepont in anger. And he struck his desk with a blow that nearly broke the lid.

Monseigneur de Roquebrun, already faint from the heat of the day, went purple with rage at this unexpected insult. 'Sir,' he said, 'during my long clerical life I have had priests who were hard and ungrateful, or immoral, but I have never had anyone like you. I heaped favours on you and you turned them all against me, making them weapons with which to wound me. To whom do you owe your membership of this court? To your bishop. And you behave here as if the charitable souls of the diocese of Lormières had done nothing for you – as if you were still a rough peasant of Harros, still driving unclean animals in the woods.'

'I am ready to repay the diocesan treasury the cost of my five years at the Seminary,' cried Tigrane, leaping up in fury at the insult.

'The diocesan court will not accept anything from you. In punishment for your savage pride I condemn you to live under the burden of the alms you have received.'

'Alms!'

'That humbles you, doesn't it? You who were sharp enough to slip into holy orders without shedding one wretched human passion. I wish the whole diocese could see you at this moment, and judge how worthy you were to receive a scholarship from it.'

'Perhaps it might also learn how worthy you were to become its bishop,' retorted Capdepont, raising a threatening arm.

Monseigneur de Roquebrun was standing. He was dumbfounded. His lips moved but did not pronouce a single word. Suddenly his face turned purple. He collapsed into his chair, stricken by apoplexy.

While everyone crowded round the Bishop, and Abbé Ternisien gave cries of grief, Capdepont calmly picked up some sheets of paper scattered on his desk, carefully folded them and then with slow steps left the diocesan court.

As Monseigneur de Roquebrun did not recover his senses, they had to move him to the bishop's palace, and send in haste for the doctors. Abbé Lavernède ran round the town, knocking on all the doors. Several practitioners came in haste, and the poor invalid was restored to some sort of consciousness.

For some hours there was great anxiety. At length Dr Leblanc, the Bishop's physician in ordinary, declared that his lordship would get over it, and that he would guarantee his recovery.

At this news the tear-stained face of Abbé Ternisien lit up with joy. The poor private secretary was warmly shaking Dr Leblanc's hand when there suddenly appeared at the Bishop's bedroom door Dr Mical, brother of the professor of moral philosophy at the Great Seminary, the intimate friend of Abbé Capdepont.

Abbé Lavernède rushed up to him. 'Sir,' he said, 'Monseigneur is grateful for your promptness, but his lordship wants no one at his bedside except his usual doctor, Monsieur Leblanc.'

'Nevertheless, I see Dr Barbaste here,' said Mical, somewhat disconcerted.

'True, sir. But he's part of the household, like Monsieur Leblanc.'

'Really?' said the poor man, who had neither his brother's wit nor his malice. 'I have just been to the Great Seminary for my daily visit, and it's Abbé Capdepont who has sent me.'

'Then tell Monsieur Capdepont that Monseigneur is quite out of danger. I'm sure the news will give him the greatest pleasure.'

While Dr Mical went downstairs Abbé Lavernède murmured between his teeth: 'What a wretch, this Capdepont! He wanted to see if he had succeeded in killing Monseigneur. Ah, Tigrane, Tigrane!'

The rumour of this sad event spread through Lormières, and all the Quarter of the Convents rushed anxiously to the bishop's palace. This crowd of discreet, polite people talking in hushed voices begged to be brought to see Monseigneur, impatient for news of him, whom they so profoundly honoured. But Monseigneur, whose muscular powers were gradually returning after a moment's suspension, made a sign of refusal, and Abbé Ternisien turned away the nobles and the faithful of the Quarter, who, moreover, went away as quietly as they had come.

All the same, the poor private secretary had not disposed of the terrible emotions of the day. About seven o'clock in the evening, at nightfall, there was a great noise near the cathedral. It was the Quarter of the Paper-Mills which after twelve hours of hard work came also for news.

Abbé Ternisien was on his way out to these worthy workers who had come with their wives and children, when the Bishop recalled him by a sign.

'What, Monseigneur! You want to see them?'

He made an affirmative sign.

'I forbid it!' said Dr Leblanc.

'It's impossible,' insisted the Vicomte de Castagnerte, for whom the bishop's palace was like an annexe of his own house, and who had been the first arrival on the scene.

Monseigneur de Roquebrun shook himself violently, then by a superhuman effort of will he freed his tongue from the paralysis that had held it captive. 'They're my poor. Let them in!' he said, very distinctly.

It was a touching and sublime sight, the presence of all these rough workers' faces in the big bedroom of the Bishops of Lormières. The men stood holding their hats, in an attitude of thought and reverence; the women on their knees as in church, praying with eyes drowned in tears; the children looking on with curiosity.

'Tell me, Monsieur Ternisien,' asked a worker, as the dense crowd was pouring out into rue St Irénée. 'Is it true that it was Monsieur Capdepont who caused the stroke?'

'Oh, dear! Who can have told you that, friend?'

'Monsieur Leblanc's servant. She heard Abbé Lavernède telling the doctor.'

'The woman is mistaken. It was just the heat that caused the trouble.'

'All the better for Monsieur Capdepont,' answered the man. 'Because we don't like him. He's a fine black beetle,* this curé of the Great Seminary.'

For these good people, Monsieur de Roquebrun and his secretary were not 'black beetles'.

After this long flashback, necessary for the complete revelation of our characters, let us hasten to rejoin Monseigneur de Roquebrun. He has just left the Paper-Mills and is going up again to the higher town by small steps.

---

* Black beetle/*calotin*: a rude word for a priest, it has no English equivalent.

V

THE PALACE GARDEN

As the Bishop of Lormières entered the rue St Irénée, at the end of which is the bishop's palace, a priest, who was rapidly coming down the street, ran up to him eagerly. 'You, at last, Monseigneur!' he said happily. 'Do you know it isn't wise to escape like that in the state you are still in?'

'Come, Ternisien! Do you think you're going to guard me under your wing till the end of the world?' said the old man good-humouredly.

'I don't want you to risk being alone in the streets,' insisted the private secretary with the touching despotism of true affection.

'*You* don't want it? . . . Ah, that's charming!'

'I know the doctors say you are cured.'

'Well, then?'

'But I . . .'

'But you, who are a fierce tyrant, want to detain me illegally.'

'I love you!' murmured Abbé Ternisien, all his heart breaking out in his words.

'Dear child!'

Monseigneur de Roquebrun took his secretary's arm and they made some steps in silence.

'Well, Monseigneur,' said the Abbé roguishly, 'are you going to tell me where you've been?'

'An inquiry into my conduct?'

'I must certainly scold you if you haven't been good.'

'Then scold me hard. I've been terrible.'

'Terrible! . . . And where was it?' asked the young priest in alarm.

'My dear child,' said the Bishop seriously. 'Justice is lame, she is as slow as a tortoise. But she gets there.'

'I'm sure you've been to the Great Seminary.'

'That's where I've come from.'

'And you didn't take me?'

'What good would that do you? Apart from the excellent Abbé Lavernède they all hate you there, and if they insulted you it would kill me.'

'No doubt that awful Capdepont . . .'

'Capdepont? You can be sure he's always the same. He's not a priest, he's a Red Indian – the sort I saw in my youth when I was a missionary in America.'

'Then why does your lordship insist on seeing this bad man all the time?'

'Why?' cried the Bishop, whose anger flared up again. 'You ask me why, Ternisien? Because he's a bad priest, and I won't have such a thing in my diocese, because I won't allow him to cut out my priests after his pattern. Finally, because I've sworn to break the pride of this really diabolic creature, and make him humble himself in front of me.'

'A hard job.'

'What do you know about it? To begin with, he's reduced to his canonry at St Irenaeus. . . . Oh, let him write to Paris if he likes. I've decided to take no precautions. I've put up with enough. At last, it's the will of God that I should show myself. . . . I've told this rebel, and the other directors, that the Fathers of Catholic Instruction will take possession of the Great Seminary in October, at the beginning of term.'

'That's strong action, Monseigneur.'

'Besides, I shan't stop there with this gentleman. I mean to hunt down his ambitious plans and prevent their realization. Don't forget that, some months ago, when I was still dangerously ill, Capdepont spread the rumour that he was going to be appointed Bishop of Lormières. He'd played the same odious comedy at the death of Monseigneur Grandin, my predecessor, and it nearly succeeded. I don't want the same scandal repeated when I am no more, and it depends on you, Ternisien, to prevent it.'

'On me, Monseigneur, on me?'

'Let's go in. I'll let you into my secret plans.'

The bishop's palace at Lormières looks like an old fortress. High, crenellated towers on the east and west flank an enormous main building, with low doors and narrow windows like loopholes, and grinning gargoyles. Although the front faces south, the palace receives rare rays of sun because the gigantic church of St Irenaeus casts shadows over it, and keeps it in a sort of eternal half-light. This exaggerates the difference in colour and preservation between the feudal entablature of the towers, which is bathed in light, and the architectural ornaments over the doors and windows of the main building. Above, in the clouds, the stone has kept the sharpness of its edges and almost its original lustre. Below, the damp daily heaps the soil with imperceptible debris, and there is not a moulding unencroached upon. The shade slowly devours the monument.

Monseigneur de Roquebrun and Ternisien entered the spacious court which extends in front of the palace and advanced towards a large glass door at the centre of the main building. An usher, always with sloped arms, opened the door, and they entered a vast room littered with books and papers.

The Bishop, evidently tired, sank into an armchair and sat silent for a few minutes. Abbé Ternisien looked at him anxiously.

'Let's go and hide in the garden,' said Monseigneur de Roquebrun suddenly. 'We shall be more by ourselves under the trees. Here we risk being disturbed.'

The private secretary, very much worried, offered his arm without a word.

They went down six steps into the beautiful garden on the west side of the palace.

Abbé Ternisien could not have misunderstood; Monseigneur de Roquebrun had very serious things to confide to him. What was he going to say?

The poor secretary almost trembled, so much was he afraid of hearing whatever it was that would take him away from his present quiet, and the delightful peace he had enjoyed for ten years with his venerable friend. Anxious to know the answer to this riddle too long concealed from him, he three times invited the Bishop to sit down under the shade of the chestnut trees. But the latter, as if afraid now of the decisive moment of explanation, took pleasure in delaying it, and walked as if carefree down the paths.

They came to the small clear stream bounding the garden on the side of the town.

'Are we to cross it?' asked Ternisien with innocent irony.

'No, no,' said the old man, and halted.

There was a bench there under the large trees. They sat down.

'My dear child,' said the Bishop. 'This morning, while you were saying your mass in the cathedral, I received a letter from Paris full of grievous news.'

'The General, perhaps?'

'No, my brother is well, thank God! It was he who wrote.'

'What is it, Monseigneur?'

'It is that, unless we take great care, Canon Capdepont will certainly be appointed Bishop.'

'What! They'd dare inflict such an affront on the Holy Father?'

'They will dare. . . . I went at once to the Great Seminary. I must get this man to compromise himself, and I think his exuberant temperament will make that easy. . . . Ternisien, it's no longer just a question of you and me, but of the Church. . . . I had decided not to talk about the coming of the Fathers of Catholic Instruction to Lormières until the day of the ordination, but the Abbé Capdepont having driven me to extremities – as he always does – I said everything. I've even allotted new posts to some of these gentlemen.'

'There'll be a row in the diocese, Monseigneur.'

'All the better! That's what I'm hoping for. If a revolution breaks out and I find the hand of Capdepont in it, he's lost.'

'Perhaps the revolution will break out, but you won't be able to manage to find your enemy's hand in it.'

'Do you think he's so clever?'

'He? No, he's too violent for that. But there are clever people at the Great Seminary.'

'Who?'

'Mical, Monseigneur. Professor Mical, the friend of Capdepont, his guide and controller. That's a man who's very subtle, and you must beware of him.'

The Bishop thought for a moment. 'Capdepont', he continued, 'probably doesn't know that he is very near getting all he has hoped for in life. After ten years of efforts and struggle to get a mitre, he is tired and giving up hope. Hence his growing anger. . . . Suppose, in the explosion of his diabolic fury, he were to provoke a scandal that reverberated as far as Paris!'

'And what bishopric is intended for the Superior of the Great Seminary?' asked the private secretary. 'I don't know of a vacancy.'

'That's the dreadful thing. They intend him for Lormières.'

'I suppose they will wait till you're dead!' cried Abbé Ternisien in anger.

'Alas, I am half dead, am I not? After one attack of apoplexy, a second . . . then the grave.'

'Oh, Monseigneur, Monseigneur!'

'When they heard my condition at the Ministry, from the mouth of General de Roquebrun himself, a very influential person who was there uttered these cruel words: "At last we can provide for Capdepont."'

'How disgraceful!'

'My brother gives me some details. In Paris they know that Capdepont has no talent for administration, and that's why his name was put aside when lately they were filling the see of St Claude, despite a genuine promise from the Empress, and the stubborn support of Monsieur Jérôme Bonnardot. But they think him capable of administering Lormières, supported by the chapter, which includes experienced men, and helped in his task by the clergy, whom he has known for thirty years. So this is the situation – Monsieur Capdepont, Bishop of Lormières after Monseigneur de Roquebrun.'

Abbé Ternisien was speechless.

The Bishop impulsively took his hands fondly in his own. 'My child,' he said, 'I'm going to ask a very great service from you.'

'A service, Monseigneur? Speak quickly, please.'

'Take care! I know your humility. Perhaps you won't accept my request.'

'Oh, Father!'

'Will you accept the heavy burden of the episcopate?'

'I, a bishop?'

'Perhaps Monsieur Bonnardot may tell Capdepont about the favourable dispositions of the Ministry towards him. In that case he'll be on his guard. Besides, as you said just now, Abbé Mical might hold him back if he wanted to let himself go in some new outrage. Then his violent character won't put him into our hands, and we must trust to other means to make it impossible for him to become a bishop. . . . Listen. . . . When I made my journey to Rome on my appointment, as I did not speak Italian, I asked Cardinal Maffeï for a French cleric able to guide me through the splendours of the Eternal City. You came, I saw you, you got on with me perfectly, and when you spoke of going back to the Franciscans at Tivoli, I talked to you about my diocese, and I carried you off. But, though far from Italy, you wisely kept up your connections with the Romans. These connections, joined with my own, and with the knowledge of my parlous state of health, will easily get the Vatican to appoint you as suffragan Bishop of Lormières. So there will be no difficulty on the part of Rome.'

'But what about Paris?'

'There we shall find some obstacles. First of all, the budget, then the firm wish of the Government not to create any more coadjutors, and then troubles with Rome. . . . We shall get through these troubles. General de Roquebrun has made a place for himself in the Senate, and he will throw all his weight into the scales on our side. He will go to the Tuileries, he'll see the Emperor, he'll dissuade the Empress, and convince the Minister. There's nothing that his zeal for religion and affection for me will make impossible to him. He'll make Capdepont known, and he'll make you known. Besides, in this serious business, I have every reason to count on the devoted help of my old friend, the Cardinal Archbishop of Lyons.'

'Really, Monseigneur, I am astonished at so much kindness and indulgence, but I beg you to keep me out of such a terrible adventure. Just now you reminded me of the Franciscan monastery at Tivoli, where you first saw me. My dream – if I could form a dream in the happiness with which you surround me – is not to rise to the episcopate, but to find my way back to my former retreat, when God takes away the protector He has given me. I have always been left cold by the splendours of earthly power, which inspire some priests with the most ardent folly. I'm not made for that.'

'I told you, child, that it's not a question of you, but of the Church.'

'And do you believe the Church will find in me the bishop she so much needs in this dreadful age through which we are passing? When have I given you the signs that I have acquired that superior virtue which could be an example to all the clergy of a diocese? When have you learned that I have a soul firm enough to govern four or five hundred priests? Haven't your ten years as a bishop enlightened you about the spirit of revolt that is breathing from every direction? The Revolution has made a breach in the Church too, and I don't feel able to cope with it. Do you want a brave heart? Take Abbé Lavernède.'

'I will quote you the words of Scripture: "You are a man of little faith." I hardly know Monsieur Lavernède, and I love you.'

'But what do you want me to do?' cried the private secretary in terror.

'I want you to put yourself in my hands, or rather those of God, who often chooses the weakest to confound the strongest. *Elegit Deus ignobilia ut confundet fortia.* . . . In your candid, angelic nature you are thinking about the good you couldn't do if you were a bishop, and forgetting the harm Capdepont would do if he became a bishop instead. Think of the efforts you and I have made together to change the condition of this unhappy diocese. Do you think Capdepont, as Bishop of Lormières, would respect our work? All these regular clergy brought here to edify a people who on the plain are very backward, and in the mountains half savage. All these nuns settled at various points to look after the sick, teach the children, help the poor – all these heroes and heroines of prayer and sacrifice who bring the blessings of Heaven on my people, what will become of them with Rufin Capdepont? Ah, if it were known what we have done for this wretched district, you and I! If they knew how much we had spent, you more than two hundred thousand francs – and I, my whole personal fortune, half a million – to endow this region without almshouses, crèches, schools, orphanages? They will know, Ternisien. I shall go and tell them in Paris.'

'Will you go to Paris, Monseigneur?'

51

'Do you think it's not worth the trouble?'

'But your health? Your health, so precious to the diocese and to me . . .'

'Don't cry, child,' said the Bishop, much moved.

'But if the journey were to tire you?'

'The journey will do me good, so long as you consent to come with me.'

'I'll go anywhere with you,' cried the private secretary.

Monseigneur de Roquebrun embraced him long and tenderly, as a father embraces his child.

In silence they returned to the palace.

VI

THE ORDINATION

Nevertheless, it was clear from the embarrassed yet cautious air of the priests who turned up at the offices of the episcopate for one reason or another that they were being stirred up against Monseigneur de Roquebrun and that a revolution would soon break out. What was this storm in a teacup going to be?

The Bishop, resolved to preserve a scornful composure towards Capdepont – a clever way of pushing the mountaineer of Harros to extreme folly – was not in the least alarmed at these secret agitations, and wittily made fun of them.

As for Abbé Ternisien, going about the town from the salon of Baronne Thévenot in the Quarter of the Paper-Mills, where they sang the praises of Capdepont, to the salon of the Vicomte de Castagnerte in the Quarter of the Convents, where everyone was devoted to Monseigneur de Roquebrun, he saw things far less optimistically. Some chance words, a very diplomatic conversation with old Clamouse, Archpriest of St Irenaeus, who was taking the side of Capdepont, his vicar in 1842, made him feel sure that the struggle would be serious.

Besides, a thousand rumours were circulating.

'Monseigneur de Roquebrun, prevented by his bad state of health from continuing to direct his diocese, has just resigned.'

'The Emperor, at the solicitation of General Comte de Roquebrun, senator, has appointed the Bishop of Lormières Canon of the Imperial Chapter at St Denis.'

'Monseigneur de Roquebrun will make his farewell to his clergy on the day of the ordination in the Great Seminary.'

'It is expected that Abbé Rufin Capdepont, whom the Empress has for a long time treated with distinction, will be called to the see of Lormières.'

Such treacherous hostility overwhelmed the poor Abbé

Ternisien and filled his life with anxiety. If the smallest of these insinuations came to his ears, Monseigneur de Roquebrun, in spite of his resolution, would be unable to accept it with calm. And what would be the result of a fresh attack on this old man, hardly recovered from paralysis? He would certainly die of it. A sinister idea came into the head of the private secretary. 'Who knows if Capdepont doesn't deliberately wish to kill his bishop?'

Ternisien, trembling, made the sign of the cross, and murmured his prayers.

The 26th May was a splendid day from the start. From seven o'clock in the morning the sun lit up the rose window of the Barnabites, whose reflections were like the red flames of a conflagration. One after another the houses of the Quarter of the Convents opened cautiously, then a few women dressed in black slipped out furtively into the street.

But the crowd grew greater and greater, so that towards eight o'clock it was almost impossible to walk in the allées St Macaire – a narrow square for that matter – at the end of which rose the high walls of the Great Seminary. The faithful of the Quarter of the Convents were not alone in crowding against this narrow surface, but a good number of workers from the Quarter of the Paper-Mills had come, dragging their wives and children with them.

'Ah, you're coming to attend the ordination, Thévenot?' cried the Vicomte de Castagnerte, seeing the former deputy, who was elbowing his way forward.

'Like everyone, I'm coming for news. . . . By the way, you who see the Bishop ought to know something?'

'I swear I know nothing, Baron. . . . Incidentally, you who see Capdepont, what have you heard?'

There was a minute's silence.

'Madame Thévenot hasn't come with you?' said Monsieur de Castagnerte.

'We've lost sight of each other. She's over there with Edmond.'

'What does the Baronne think of the situation?'

'She thinks Rufin Capdepont would make a superb bishop, and I'm of her opinion. He's a proud man, that priest. I've made a study of him.'

'He's done as much by you,' answered the Vicomte subtly.

All at once the two leaves of the big gate of the Great Seminary, which give on the allées St Macaire, opened. The crowd rushed forward and was swallowed up.

The huge nave of the Gothic chapel of the Minims was cut in two by a high wooden balustrade. The faithful of Lormières respectfully stopped at the balustrade and, like people used to going to church, sat down silently, without coughing, on the long rows of chairs set to receive them.

A bell rang.

The ordinands, some in surplices, some in white albs, invaded the choir, and two by two, with measured steps, they advanced to the reserved part of the nave to take their places. First came the young students who were to receive the tonsure; next those for minor orders; then those about to take the redoubtable step of the subdeaconate; then the candidates for the deaconate, and lastly the aspirants to the priesthood.

They all fell on their knees.

The bell rang a second time.

At the same moment a hurried crowd of minor clergy of every age and appearance poured into the church from the two wide-open doors of the sacristy. There were gentle, naïve faces, other faces rough and hollow-cheeked, dark and fair heads – all of them went like a flock of sheep towards the simple school benches lined up on the left, and they established themselves as well as they could.

'Mercy! What's the meaning of this avalanche?' said Monsieur de Castagnerte. 'Have all of the curates of the diocese arranged to meet here?'

'I told you there would be news, Vicomte,' said Thévenot, rubbing his hands with satisfaction.

'Be quiet, gentlemen,' said the Baronne turning round. 'I can't say my prayers.'

'For Capdepont, no doubt?' asked Monsieur de Castagnerte maliciously.

The master of ceremonies sounded the bell a third time.

The directors of the Great Seminary appeared. A few paces behind them walked the Superior, solitary and grave.

Abbé Capdepont halted at the foot of the high altar, and while his colleagues went to sit down in the fine stalls of massive oak on the right in the extension of the choir, he said a short prayer. His attitude was noble, collected, solemn. He blessed himself devoutly, then in turn walked to his seat. Passing the clergy of the diocese, crowded on the wooden benches, he imperceptibly nodded his head. The others bowed profoundly. He paid no attention to this.

'Handsome, isn't he?' exclaimed Baron Thévenot.

'I find his manner rather insolent,' answered Monsieur de Castagnerte. 'Ah,' he added, 'I hear my horses.'

In fact an old barouche, adorned with the arms of the Vicomte, harnessed to two Basque horses that seemed to have difficulty in drawing it, had just stopped in the allées St Macaire.

'Monseigneur!' cried a beadle.

The ordinands, heads bowed, arms crossed over their chests, walked in procession towards the back of the church.

Some of the minor clergy fidgeted, in obvious desire to go towards their bishop; but repressed by Capdepont's eyes upon them, they did not dare leave their places, and sat down again, crestfallen.

Nevertheless, Monseigneur de Roquebrun, getting down from the carriage with his two vicars-general and his private secretary, waited at the threshold of the church of the Minims for the Superior of the Great Seminary to come to offer him holy water, according to custom, and no one moved.

Abbé Lavernède, indignant at such an unspeakable lack of respect, bravely left his stall. 'Gentlemen,' he said, taking a step towards the minor clergy, who were fascinated by Capdepont's look, 'we are priests, and as such we owe homage to our bishop. I will walk at your head. Come.'

The crowd of clergy, accustomed to obey, broke ranks at once and walked after the professor of sacred eloquence.

Abbé Mical, with his little blinking eye, had followed all this business. Frightened of scandal and fearing a scene even in the chapel, for the Bishop was not long-suffering, he pushed Rufin Capdepont and managed to prise him out of his place. Unfortunately when they arrived at the holy-water font his lordship had already intoned *Veni Creator*, and the procession in two columns was singing as it returned to the choir.

The ceremony began at once. Such haste astonished the clergy, and the faithful at the back of the church, who were used to hearing the Bishop address some words of welcome and encouragement to the young tonsured clerks. Oh, no doubt he would speak to the future subdeacons.

Monseigneur de Roquebrun conferred the minor orders without turning his attention away from the *Rituale* open in front of him; and when the subdeacons, their hearts full and eyes wet with tears at the moment before making the final step which would throw them into the sacred ministry for life, awaited a consoling word, the Bishop, standing on the steps of the high altar, contented himself with saying in a laconic voice: *Huc accedite* – 'Come here!'

It was clear that Monseigneur de Roquebrun, moved by the insult offered to him at the door of the chapel, was in a hurry to finish the ceremony. The most holy of men could not escape some preoccupations, and the glances which the Bishop directed towards the minor clergy, crowded on the left of the choir, proved that the unaccustomed presence of so many priests had wounded him.

Was it a conspiracy? What did they want of him?

Twice, in the middle of the ordination, he wanted to summon the Superior of the Great Seminary to ask him for the reason for such a concourse of clergy. Even old Clamouse, almost crippled, and only seen at long intervals in his position in the cathedral, had found the strength to come here! It was unbelievable.

But Abbé Ternisien, standing on the right of Monseigneur de Roquebrun, calmed him, held him back, controlled him.

'Jesus Christ is there on the altar, ready to be sacrificed,' whispered this pious priest in his ear. 'Let us suffer, as He has suffered.' Then he murmured: 'Your health, Monseigneur, your health! Remember that we have to leave for Paris tomorrow.'

The Bishop smiled through his anger, and contained himself prudently.

When the ordination was finished, Monseigneur de Roquebrun, preceded by his vicars-general and his private secretary and Abbé Lavernède, went to the sacristy. He

57

quickly took off his pontifical vestments.

'I'll run and order the carriage, Monseigneur,' said Abbé Ternisien.

'The carriage! Not yet. It is the custom that on the day of the ordination I should distribute some cures to the young clergy who have received the priesthood. Why should I not follow the custom? Do you think I am afraid of the regiment of priests collected here without my orders? Besides, I have promised the directors to whom I have not yet been able to give posts, to assign them to them today . . .'

'Perhaps your lordship could wait,' ventured Lavernède.

'Wait for my clergy to put a foot on my throat and stifle me, isn't that true? Monsieur Lavernède, you know better than I that this is a duel to the death. It is horrible to think that such fearful strife can break out in the sanctuary, in the presence of God. But look, can I retreat? . . . After my thanksgiving I shall rejoin these gentlemen in the conference chamber. Tell them this, if you please.'

'Monseigneur! Monseigneur!' stammered Ternisien.

'My child, it isn't comfortable to be a bishop, but when God has chosen us, we must do Him honour to the end.'

He fell on his knees at a prie-dieu.

Everyone went away, seized with respect.

VII

THE PRINCE OF DARKNESS

While Monseigneur de Roquebrun recited the prayers that like any simple priest he always recited after celebrating mass, Abbé Capdepont, at the head of the directors of the Great Seminary and all the clergy who had come to the ordination, went to the conference chamber.

The crowd noisily invaded the stalls of the Minims and jostled each other.

'Gentlemen,' cried Capdepont, rising on the steps of the abbot's throne, 'respect the hierarchy. Only the beneficed clergy have the right to the stalls. The curates will take the benches at the back of the room.'

The Superior had spoken. The priests-in-charge gave up the seats they had improperly taken.

'Gentlemen,' continued Capdepont, in a voice he forced himself to control, though suppressed anger made it all the more resonant, 'I am not at all satisfied with your attitude in the chapel. The Archpriest Clamouse, the priest in this diocese most eminent for virtue and learning, holds in his hands a long request signed by all of you, in which you express to your bishop your discontent with the way – peculiar to say the least – in which he treats his clergy. Have you forgotten that the regulars, like a rain of locusts, have come down on our parishes, and that the Fathers of Catholic Instruction are going to turn out from here your former masters, who are so good and devoted? If you have forgotten this, what is the meaning of your presence here? And if you remember, how is it that just now – on the prompting of Abbé Lavernède, whom the marked favours of the Bishop have moved to neglect his duty to me, his superior – you went this morning before the ordination to greet him whom you accused of trampling on you, and on whom, you said, you were determined to inflict a

59

lesson? It would have been well that from his entrance into our chapel, Monseigneur de Roquebrun had learned that his clergy is on the point of estrangement from him, and that, to use the language of politics, if he makes a *coup d'état*, we are ready to reply with a revolution.'

'He shall know, he shall know!' interrupted the trembling voice of the Archpriest Clamouse.

'Yes, yes, he shall know!' cried the crowd of priests, raising their arms in anger.

'Besides, you must consider', went on Capdepont, 'that all of us here are equally compromised in our bishop's eyes. Even if we didn't know his violent character, his silence during the ordination ceremony would be enough to tell us the thoughts of vengeance that must excite him. So, when he appears, no weakness! Instead of bending your heads under the yoke, pull yourselves up with strength and dignity. In fact, what can be done against you? Nothing, absolutely nothing. A priest who revolts, even against injustice, is suspended. Two hundred can't be. If you are firm, Monseigneur de Roquebrun, faced with a formidable opposition, will leave the diocese, and perhaps Heaven, in clemency towards us, will send us someone to put things straight.'

'Count on us, Superior, count on us!' exclaimed the curés in the stalls and the minor clergy on the benches.

The door of the conference chamber half opened, and through the crack passed the sly head of Abbé Mical. 'Silence!' he whispered. 'Here's the Bishop!'

After such an explosion of hostile sentiments, those who have not had the chance to study priests will without doubt imagine that the clergy of Lormières made a very circumspect and cold welcome to their bishop when he entered the Great Seminary. Nothing of the kind. On the appearance of Monseigneur de Roquebrun, lined faces became smooth by a sort of enchantment, and on many there beamed a sort of hypocritical and sanctimonious smile, the smile of servitude.

It is surprising that Rufin Capdepont, whose profound study of history ought to have taught him something about human nature, had not considered, before attempting this impious rising against legitimate authority, that the exercise of liberty requires apprenticeship, and that one does not give up

60

the habits of a slave because one has written one's name on a sheet of paper. But now, as always when it was his own business, passion had blinded him. The peasant of Harros, the man of instinct, ruined all the fine and daring plans of Abbé Capdepont, and made them miscarry.

Monseigneur de Roquebrun came forward, leaning on the arm of his private secretary. He was no doubt tired after the long ceremony of the ordination, for he sat down and remained silent, in a state of exhaustion.

The old Abbé Clamouse, prompted by a wink from Rufin Capdepont, rose painfully. Helped by Abbé Mical he dragged himself to the middle of the conference chamber. 'Would Monseigneur allow me to address a few words to him?' he groaned in a die-away voice.

'I am listening to you, Archpriest.'

Monsieur Clamouse coughed, and adjusted his spectacles on the end of his hooked nose, dirty with snuff, and unrolled a long piece of paper. He screeched his words.

'Monseigneur, the clergy of your diocese feel the greatest grief at the encroachment, daily greater, by the religious corporations . . .'

The Bishop rose quickly to his feet. 'Stop, sir, you are not speaking to me. You are reading, I think . . .'

'No doubt,' stammered the Archpriest in a flurry.

'And where have you found that you are allowed to address remonstrances to your bishop?'

'But Monseigneur . . .'

'Is it in the treatises of ecclesiastical discipline or in canon law? It seems to me, on the contrary, that Thomassin in his writings forbids these improper demonstrations.'

'It is only a petition about the regulars . . .'

'I do not wish to hear it. If you had any remark to make relative to the acts of my administration, why did you not take the trouble to come to the palace? Haven't I received you a hundred times? And when have I ceased to pay you the deference due to your long priesthood which, more than once, I have mentioned in my Great Seminary as an example to the young clerics? Since my enthronement in this see of Lormières my door has been wide open not only to you, sir, but to all my priests, to the humblest as to the highest in the hierarchy. If there is one I have refused to welcome, let him rise and accuse me.'

'I am very sorry, Monseigneur,' stammered Monsieur Clamouse, trembling. 'And I ask your pardon.'

'You are absolved, Archpriest. When you walked this way this morning, in spite of the infirmity that should have kept you in your parish, I wish to believe that you didn't quite know what you were going to do here. But *another* knew in your place. It was a question of administering a terrible blow to your bishop, and it was desired that it should be the most respected priest in the diocese who struck the blow. Think — Monseigneur de Roquebrun reprimanded by the Archpriest Clamouse in front of a great number of clergy, a fine sight! Happily, in spite of their faults and unworthiness, God watches over those to whom He has committed the protection of His Church, and God has not allowed that a satanic plot, in which without your knowledge you have been involved, should succeed through your co-operation. God has had pity on your sixty years of virtue, of sacrifice to His glory. It is He who has snatched you from the hands of the tempter.'

Little bright tears watered the shrivelled cheeks of the old Archpriest. He went forward to the abbot's throne, and when he reached the first step he bent both knees.

Monseigneur de Roquebrun came down to him and tried to lift him.

'Ah, no!' murmured Monsieur Clamouse. 'Bless me, Monseigneur, for I have sinned.'

The Bishop solemnly raised his hands.

When the Archpriest was standing again, Monseigneur de Roquebrun was in front of him, looking at him, and quite shaken.

Suddenly, carried away by a generous motion of the heart, the two old men fell into each other's arms and closely embraced one another. A thrill went through the crowd. Here and there one heard strangled sobs.

Abbé Mical made a hideous face.

As for Abbé **Capdepont**, his features had taken on a marble rigidity. He stood in his stall, motionless and cold as a statue.

The Bishop reappeared on the abbot's throne, his face radiant with a holy joy. 'Archpriest,' he said, with penetrating emotion, 'this day which they wished to make so sad for me, you have made the happiest of my episcopate. In embracing you, I felt I was embracing my whole diocese, and I thrilled with happiness. . . . My God!' he added, also shedding tears. 'My God, tell me what I must do to be loved? It is so sweet to be loved . . .'

'You are loved, Monseigneur, you are loved!' cried all the conference chamber, moved by an irresistible tenderness.

'You will all come to see me at the palace. You'll tell me my faults, the mistakes I've made, and henceforth we shall be a united family . . .'

'Yes, we'll come, we'll all come.'

'I shall be a father to my children till death,' continued the Bishop, showing nakedly his love-starved heart. 'It's not just a question of the religious orders that I'm ready to decide in your favour, if I'm shown that their presence in this diocese is in any way prejudicial to my clergy. Besides, why did I call the regulars here? Why have I established some of them in the remotest corners of our mountains unless it is for them to help my priests in preaching, in teaching children, and in the administration of the sacraments? I was not seeking enemies for you, but devoted friends, ready to give you help at all times in the work of our holy religion. Certainly the parish clergy have given me abundant proof of zeal, but there is more than one place where their efforts have failed. Must I give an example? At Harros, the home of the eminent Abbé Capdepont, for years the divine seed was falling on stone. The Marists came, they trenched in this rebellious soil, and now it bears a plentiful harvest, *messis multa*. . . . And then, being priests, why not remember that it is in the religious communities that it is easiest to practise the exercises recommended by the holy councils for attaining Christian perfection?'

Monseigneur de Roquebrun paused for a moment. Abbé Ternisien leaned towards him, and they exchanged a few words.

'Gentlemen, those of you who have just received the priesthood,' said the private secretary. 'Monseigneur, who needs a moment's rest, asks me to tell you the cures to which his lordship is pleased to call you.'

63

He read quite a long list. He had hardly finished when, with a gigantic effort, the Bishop rose to his feet. 'I was', he said, 'to assign posts today to some of the directors of the Great Seminary, but after what has just passed I feel full of hesitation. Since here all hearts are somewhat strained, who knows if I shall do better to break off the negotiations begun with the Fathers of Catholic Instruction?' Suddenly, turning towards Capdepont, he asked: 'What do you think of breaking off in this way, Superior?' he said.

'I think, Monseigneur, if there is an engagement, the engagement should be kept.'

'But if the matter has not been definitely settled?'

'In that case, you would be free as far as the Fathers of Catholic Instruction are concerned, but not as far as we, the directors of this establishment, are concerned.'

'Why so?'

'Have you not assigned posts to Monsieur Mical, Monsieur Turlot and Monsieur Lavernède? Have you not enjoined me to occupy my stall in the chapter of St Irenaeus?'

'You would not like to retain the direction of the Great Seminary?'

'As you yourself have relieved me of my functions, probably you had serious reasons for doing so.'

'Well, if I wished to keep you in the situation you so long occupied?'

'To my great regret, I should find myself obliged to refuse this favour.'

'This is a firm resolution. When your bishop has made two steps towards you, you refuse to make one towards him?'

'I respect my bishop.'

There had been enough advances; once more, Monseigneur de Roquebrun had touched with a finger the bottom of his untameable character – a hard and icy stone.

'Come, Monsieur Capdepont. . . . Come, Superior,' those present could not help crying, inviting him to respect, and to concessions.

'What do you want, all of you?' answered this sullen man, pulling himself up to his full height, and giving a look of haughty contempt at the clergy who surrounded him.

'*Beati pacifici*, Superior!' interjected old Clamouse.

'*Beati pauperes Spiritu*, Archpriest!' snapped Capdepont, ready for any sort of outburst.

'Gentlemen,' said the Bishop, struggling against the anger that again was inflaming his blood, 'the most terrible punishment that God has inflicted on the Prince of Darkness is that He has forbidden him to love – so St Theresa tells us.'

'Monseigneur!' cried Capdepont, whose eyes darted flame.

The Bishop stretched out his arm as in the ceremony of exorcism when devils are cast out, and without a word left the conference chamber.

All the priests, minor clergy and others, followed Monseigneur de Roquebrun.

Only the Abbés Capdepont and Mical did not accompany him down the vast corridors of the Minims' monastery. They remained in their stalls as if turned to stone.

'We've been tricked!' said Mical at last, coming out of his stupor.

'The imbeciles! The cowards!' said Capdepont with a gesture of despair. 'Ah, if I'm ever their bishop . . .'

'You'll revenge yourself?'

'Come, let us go out. I feel stifled.'

They went out to breathe fresh air under the shady elms in the courtyard.

VIII

THE MASS OF THE HOLY GHOST

Before leaving the Great Seminary, where their mission was decidedly over, the directors decided to celebrate a mass of the Holy Ghost. This sung mass, to which all in the secret at Lormières were to be invited, was to be like a final protest against the acts of episcopal authority.

Apart from Abbé Lavernède who, the day after the ordination, had gone without any fuss to take over the chaplaincy of the prisons, and who in consequence took no part in this sort of cabal, all the directors were present. Everyone cried out against the Bishop, who some days before had gone to Lyons with Abbé Ternisien; and it was firmly resolved to unite in invocation of the Holy Ghost before separating.

On 4th June, a week after the ordination, at ten o'clock in the morning Abbé Capdepont would go up to the altar, followed by the Abbés Mical and Turlot in the dalmatics of deacon and subdeacon, to add to the pomp of the ceremony.

On the day of the farewells, so cleverly contrived to hurt the Bishop, at the moment when Abbé Capdepont was about to join his assembled colleagues, Baron Thévenot stopped him on the threshold of the conference chamber.

'What's the matter?' asked the Canon abruptly.

'Monseigneur de Roquebrun isn't at Lyons.'

'Where is he, then?'

'He's been in Paris since four days ago.'

'In Paris?'

'I've just got that out of the Vicomte de Castagnerte.'

At this unexpected news Capdepont, though a strong and energetic man, felt a shock that made him stagger. He had to support himself on the arms of Monsieur Thévenot and of Abbé Mical. They took him back to his room.

66

'It's to oppose me that the Bishop has gone to Paris. It's to oppose me!' he cried, with the power of divination that a great passion gives. 'And when I think that while he is acting, I'm amusing myself with plotting these wretched little teases! What a pity!'

Quickly he turned his irritated face towards Abbé Mical.

'Look at the adventures you let me in for, with your hypocritical plans. When will you stop giving me advice? When will you give me the satisfaction of not meddling in any way with my affairs? If I hadn't listened to you, I should have been in Paris for a week, and what business wouldn't I have done already! But no, at the moment when I ought to have gone to the place where all my interests call me, I had the weakness to consult you once more and, naturally, caught in the mesh of your subtle reasonings, I stayed here. Now you see what's happened. Bishop Roquebrun has seen his brother the General, and they've gone together to the Tuileries. . . . What haven't they said about me to the Emperor, and still more to the Empress!'

He took a few steps, and seizing Abbé Mical, who was too weak to resist him and bent like a reed under his hand, 'Take care!' he said, devouring him with a fierce look.

Monsieur Thévenot intervened, in fear. But Abbé Mical pushed him aside. 'Don't be afraid, Baron,' he murmured. 'He won't kill me.'

'And why shouldn't I kill you?' retorted Capdepont, so confused in mind that he unconsciously showed all the perversity of his instincts.

'Because you want to be a bishop. And if you took it into your head to kill me, my corpse might give you some trouble.'

Abbé Capdepont, finding that no reply came to his lips, gave a forced laugh, which covered his face with a really frightful expression.

Monsieur Thévenot looked at him with uneasy curiosity – he believed that he was going mad – and escaped.

The terrible Canon, entirely obsessed with his anxieties, did not notice the Baron's departure. He remained in thought, with his pointed chin resting on the palm of his hand.

Suddenly he got up, and his look had that fixity which is so striking in people suffering from hallucination. . . . He walked twice round the large room . . . he stopped short and remained motionless for a few moments, as if rooted to the floor. His features, on which by will-power he had cultivated an austere serenity compatible with the priestly character, were now twisted by inward convulsions, and made him unrecognizable. His forehead, that great field where his strong intellect expanded, was now particularly afflicted. Everywhere there were lines, holes, crevices, ruins. His head, man's heavenly city, now that Capdepont was suffering the martyrdom of a mad ambition, exhibited the ravages of a terrible earthquake.

'When, on the day after the ordination,' he said slowly, as if talking to himself, 'I heard the Bishop had gone to Lyons, I wasn't without fear, though I knew of his former relations with the archbishop of that town. After the illness of Monseigneur de Roquebrun, from which he had hardly recovered, this journey seemed to me strange, to say the least. . . . Everything is now clear. The Bishop was going to Paris – only, instead of going by Bordeaux, he went by Lyons. . . . But why did that little Abbé Ternisien, when he was asked by the vicars-general, who might have had urgent matters to communicate to the Bishop, answer: 'We're going to Lyons?''

'Well, didn't they stop at Lyons?' interrupted Mical.

'What does that matter? The object of their journey was Paris . . . Abbé Ternisien has studied diplomacy in Rome, where reside the masters of this science, which is not very Christian but very Catholic. And Abbé Ternisien has made fun of us. He hasn't told lies. Oh no! But he hasn't told the truth. . . . Mical, I don't like this little Italian, all honey and sugar. When I lived in Paris I saw a lot of priests who had come back from across the mountains after a long stay. Well, I never knew one who hadn't caught a strong taint of Machiavellianism there. Machiavelli is all Italy, and Ternisien has been stamped with the common trademark.'

'Well, what are you going to do about it?'

'It's very simple. I shall leave for Paris tonight.'

'Another piece of folly.'

'Really, one could wring your neck. I'd stake my life you have some more absurd advice to give me.'

'You need fear nothing of the sort,' answered Mical coldly. 'While you go to Paris, I shall go to my new post at

Bastide-sur-Mont. I can very well give up the idea of being vicar-general, as you are giving up that of being bishop.'

He walked firmly to the door and was just going to open it when Capdepont, prey to some mad fear, turned the key and locked it.

'Will you explain yourself? Will you explain yourself?'

'What's the use? . . . . I'd rather go away.'

'You won't get out of here till I have seen all you've got in mind.'

'You wish this absolutely?'

'I insist on it.'

'Well, I think if Abbé Ternisien has too much diplomacy, you haven't enough. My advice, for which you reproach me mercilessly, has made you the Superior of the Great Seminary, Vicar-General and a serious candidate for the episcopate. They'll make you a bishop if you listen to it to the end. I say, with more sorrow than pride, I don't know what would have become of you without me. Who knows if by now all the violence and folly I have prevented wouldn't have caused you to be suspended, and perhaps unfrocked!'

'Enough! Enough!'

'You owe me something for the obstinacy with which I have saved you from yourself. But you were superior to me in intelligence, I admired you. You were my friend, I was proud of you, I loved you!'

Abbé Mical stopped, too much moved to continue.

Rufin Capdepont went back a step; his deeper nature had felt a blow. He returned towards his friend, and this rough man in whom an irresistible passion had dried up the source of sentiment, had a flash of sensibility. 'Mical,' he said in a voice that almost trembled, 'I've often been unjust to you. I beg your pardon.'

They embraced like brothers.

When they had dried their eyes, the two priests sat down near each other on the sofa.

'Well,' said the Canon in a coaxing tone, though still a prey to his demon. 'What ought I to do?'

'You ought to remain in Lormières . . . suppose the Bishop – which is very probable after the terrible alarm he has suffered – has gone to Paris simply to finish his long convalescence in the bosom of his family? Your journey north is absolutely useless. More – after the letter which Monsieur Bonnardot wrote you in August, on learning what state Monseigneur de Roquebrun was in, I think the journey could only do you harm. Have you forgotten the terms of that long letter? Monsieur Bonnardot said: "It is no good to delude yourself with visionary hopes: if you are appointed bishop, you will only be made bishop of Lormières. Here they have got used to thinking that you have some claims to that see, but you must not think of any other. They have some doubts about your aptitude for administration, and the Government has the sense not to transfer you to a diocese where you are not known, and where in consequence from the very beginning you may come up against great difficulties. Besides, why be so impatient? Monseigneur de Roquebrun's attack of apoplexy tells you, does it not, that your day is near?"'

'That's all very well. But if Bishop Roquebrun, whom I've taken no trouble to appease, has gone to Paris with the intent to do me harm? Doesn't the secrecy in which he wrapped himself up at his departure give us cause for fear?'

'Even in that case,' said Mical in a tone of conviction, 'you ought not to go away from here. Have you thought of the situation you would have to face if at the Ministry or the Tuileries – where I'm not sure that you would be received – you found yourself face to face with the hostility of your bishop? Are you simple enough to think you would win in a struggle on the slippery floor of the bureau? Your violent character leaves me in no doubt. Allow me to say again, what I've said to you a hundred times: in spite of your high ability, your gift of speech and your really noble presence, you are the last man in the world to come with honour out of a difficult situation. You have no suppleness, no aptitude. You'll lose your temper, you'll be eloquent and splendid in indignation, but you'll destroy yourself. I'm not worth anything like as much as you. But I could have been a bishop, while for ten years you kicked your heels. Life, particularly Church life, is indirect. You have to look at it both ways, to Rome and to Paris. Ask Machiavel-Ternisien.'

'So, I must let Bishop Roquebrun misinterpret my life, my character?'

70

'Ah, between you and me, do you think the poor Bishop so base?'

'Has he won you over, perhaps, by giving you the cure of Bastide-sur-Mont?' asked Capdepont, with cruel irony.

'Not at all. He's been very disagreeable towards me. But let's confess, now we're alone, that it's a good deal for your sake that we've painted him so black.'

Capdepont stood up nervously. 'I shall go by express tonight.'

'A last piece of advice. Wait. At least don't go to Paris till Monseigneur de Roquebrun is back.'

'I shall go this evening.'

'Very well. We'll take the same train as far as Bastide-sur-Mont. Goodbye to grandeur for us!'

There was a violent bang on the door. Capdepont went to open it.

'Why am I being disturbed?' he asked harshly.

'Superior,' stammered Abbé Turlot, 'there's a telegraph boy below who has a telegram from Paris for you.'

Capdepont, forgetting his usual quiet and majestic demeanour, rushed downstairs. He took the bit of blue paper from the postman and tore it open. All his face was lit up with a sort of radiance. 'Gentlemen,' he said. He could say no more, being stifled with emotion.

'Well?' asked the directors, coming scared out of the conference chamber.

Abbé Capdepont went into the room; by an effort at self-control he recovered the calm that had nearly deserted him and gravely ascended the steps of the abbot's throne. 'My friends,' he said, 'Heaven has thrown its thunderbolt. I have terrible news from Paris. I shall read you the telegram: "Monseigneur de Roquebrun died yesterday, after a second attack of apoplexy. You are appointed capitular Vicar-General. You will receive letters from the Ministry tomorrow. Above all, don't leave the diocese. Good hopes for the rest. Jérôme Bonnardot."'

'"The rest" means the bishopric for you, doesn't it, Superior?' asked Abbé Turlot.

'We shall have the bishop of our choice!' cried Abbé Mical.

'And we shan't leave the Great Seminary,' said Turlot,

71

rubbing his hands.

'Gentlemen, don't let us break into idle talk,' said Abbé Capdepont, dominating everything with his voice and his authoritative gestures. 'The moment to act has come. The Abbé Mical has pronounced the vital word. If the priests, if all the priests of the diocese recommend me to the *choice* of the Government, no doubt the Government will choose me. Ten years ago a petition in my favour was signed, but there was no general support and no result was obtained. Let the past be a lesson to you, for it matters more to you than to me. . . .'

He was out of breath, and had to pause for a moment.

'Now I must admit to you, my dear colleagues,' he went on in a smooth voice that no one had ever heard him use before, 'that it is not without a profound feeling of fear that I should accept the episcopate. What a crushing responsibility in times so difficult as ours! If ever I resign myself to it, it will be because I am moved by the hope that in this diocese, fallen into so many vicissitudes, I can restore and repair everything and *ea quae corruerant instaurabo*, as the prophet Amos says. In any case, God grant that they don't send us another man from the North!'

'We intend you to be our bishop, and you shall be!' said Abbé Mical forcibly.

'You shall be!' repeated all the directors.

Rufin Capdepont had cast his eyes up. 'God's will be done in all things,' he murmured piously. Then, in a deliberate voice he said: 'I shall go directly to the palace, to take the affairs of the diocese in hand.'

'And the mass of the Holy Ghost?' inquired Turlot.

'It won't take place, as you are not leaving this house.'

He came down from the abbot's throne. The directors bowed with shameful servility; they saw him already as their bishop. He passed proudly through the midst of them on the arm of Abbé Mical, and went out without looking at them.

72

IX

THE VICOMTE DE CASTAGNERTE

When towards evening the news of Monseigneur de Roquebrun's death spread through Lormières, there was general
consternation. In the Quarter of the Convents the churches
were full of the faithful, crowding to pray for the late bishop.
Among these pious people, of whom a part were already
unconsciously under the yoke of Capdepont, prayer was the
natural reaction to every sadness, every grief.

Grief was less pious in the Quarter of the Paper-Mills, but
was more human. At the first news that Monseigneur de
Roquebrun had died in Paris the factories shut, and men,
women and children scattered in the streets, anxious,
distressed and full of sorrow.

'Who will feed my poor old invalid parents now?' sobbed a
poor working woman, her face wet with tears.

'When I think that Monseigneur paid for the doctor and all
the medicine when my wife and children were ill, and went on
giving me ready money,' murmured a paper-maker, shaken
with emotion.

'Long live Monseigneur!' cried the little children, not
understanding what was going on.

At ten o'clock the next day a dense crowd suddenly invaded
the square of St Irenaeus. The previous evening the Vicomte de
Castagnerte had gone to the Quarter of the Paper-Mills, where
he rarely appeared, and had announced that a grand funeral
service for Monseigneur de Roquebrun would be held in the
cathedral.

The crowd was restless and the murmurs were loud. Tired of
waiting, some of them went into the church. But surprise was
at its height when they saw that nothing had been made ready
for the ceremony. No catafalque in the nave, and no black
hangings on the vast walls.

The Vicomte de Castagnerte pushed his way through to the sacristy.

There old Clamouse, having said his daily low mass, was quietly taking off his vestments. His limbs being almost numbed by his great age, he was helped by the usual sacristan, with whom was the excellent Abbé Lavernède, come as if by chance to St Irenaeus.

'Well, Archpriest,' said Monsieur de Castagnerte. 'The people are there and are beginning to get impatient.'

'My dear Vicomte, you see I'm occupied. . . . What would you do? I'm not the master . . . the people must be sent away.'

'So, the service that yesterday you promised to celebrate, won't take place?'

'Yesterday I promised, that's true. But I have since been made aware that I was exceeding my powers.'

'What!' cried the old gentleman, hardly keeping his indignation in check. 'You are the parish priest of this church and you haven't the right to say a mass for the dead without permission?'

'Yes, certainly. . . . But Vicomte, this mass is not quite like any other . . .'

'No,' retorted Monsieur de Castagnerte, clenching his teeth. 'This mass is for Monseigneur de Roquebrun, your benefactor. Was it not he who appointed you Archpriest of St Irenaeus, and Dean of the chapter of this cathedral?'

Monsieur Clamouse made no reply. He slowly folded the amice he had just taken off.

'Well,' insisted the Vicomte, 'what must be said to these poor people who have not gone to work today in order to pay a last homage to their benefactor?'

'Quite simple,' answered Monsieur Clamouse. 'Tell them to go away. . . . Besides, if the capitular Vicar-General of the diocese, Monsieur Capdepont, were to authorize the service for which you ask, at eleven o'clock you wouldn't find a priest in Lormières who hasn't said his mass yet.'

'I beg your pardon, Archpriest,' broke in Abbé Lavernède. 'There is still one. It is I.'

Old Clamouse looked at the chaplain of the prisons with an eye sparkling with malice. 'You're a "slyboots"!' he said.

'If "slyboots" means a man with a heart, you're right sir,'

74

said Monsieur de Castagnerte with an ironic smile.

The Archpriest went to the prie-dieu beside the big oak vestment chest and began to recite his thanksgiving.

'Hurry quickly to the office of the episcopate,' said Abbé Lavernède to the Vicomte. 'You'll find Monsieur Capdepont there. You were too close a friend of Monseigneur de Roquebrun for him to refuse you permission to have a great service for the dead in his honour.'

'It seems to me that we could do very well without the permission of this eternal Capdepont.'

'Perhaps. But it costs us so little not to offend a man who loses his temper on the smallest pretext. Besides, who knows if he would like to give the absolution himself?'

'That would annoy me very much!'

'Go, my good friend. . . . Meanwhile I shall calm the murmurs of the people, who are becoming angry. And I'll get everything ready for the ceremony.'

The moment that Monsieur de Castagnerte opened the door of the court of the bishop's palace, he passed Baron Thévenot on the threshold.

'Ha, you here, Vicomte!' said he. 'Whither away so fast?'

'Is Monsieur Capdepont in the office?'

'He's settled in there since yesterday. But you're not going to see him, I suppose?'

'Why shouldn't I go to see him?'

'Oh, my dear friend, he's in a temper.'

'Oh, I know it's a fierce animal, but it hasn't eaten you. . . .'

He stepped forward, but Thévenot held him back: 'Really, I understand the anger of Monsieur Capdepont. Do you know Monseigneur de Roquebrun hasn't played fair with him?'

'My dear sir,' interrupted Monsieur de Castagnerte, not without some haughtiness. 'Say what you like about Monsieur Capdepont, whom you and your wife should know profoundly. As for Monseigneur de Roquebrun, I ask you to speak of him with more respect. I had the honour to know him. He was a saint!'

He waved goodbye, and turned to the right, to the little isolated building where were the offices of the episcopate.

Monsieur de Castagnerte knocked on a door on the ground floor.

75

'Come in!' cried a shrill voice, easily recognizable as that of Abbé Mical. The old gentleman lifted a heavy latch of wrought iron. 'Abbé Capdepont?' he asked.

'What do you want of him, sir?' cried the capitular Vicar-General himself, standing up in this low room where the sun's rays never entered.

This rude welcome a little disconcerted Monsieur de Castagnerte, who was used to the exquisite manners of Monseigneur de Roquebrun, which reminded him of the former court where he had lived. However, he composed himself. 'If Abbé Capdepont is there,' he answered delicately, 'I should be glad of the honour of speaking to him for a moment.'

'Here he is, Vicomte,' said Mical, who had understood, and with a gesture he pointed to the fierce abbé.

'I beg your pardon, Vicar-General,' said the old man. 'It's so dark in this room that I didn't see you . . . as you are henceforth at the head of this diocese, I come to ask you to authorize the holding of a service.'

'For your friend, Bishop Roquebrun?' said Rufin Capdepont sharply.

'You are right, sir: for my noble friend Monseigneur the Marquis Gabriel Armand de Roquebrun, Bishop of Lormières.'

'It's not the time for this ceremony. We'll see later.'

'Kindly consider, sir, that all the workers in the paper-mills. . . .'

'It is the business of those who called the workers to St Irenaeus to take the trouble to rid our cathedral of them.'

'*Our* cathedral. . . . Confound it, Abbé, it seems that one gets used to episcopal language quickly!'

'Are you trying to insinuate by that that I'm unworthy to exercise the episcopate?'

'God forbid! But if you should become our bishop, I only hope you won't make us regret your predecessor too much.'

'Bishop Roquebrun was my enemy!' cried the peasant of Harros, whose blood was boiling.

'You are mistaken, sir. You were his!' answered Monsieur de Castagnerte with haughty dignity.

'Do you want proof?'

'I warn you, it will have to be irrefutable.'

'Listen to this letter: "His first visit to the Ministry was a mortal blow to your candidature. How could they deny him the nomination of his secretary as coadjustor when, the day before, General de Roquebrun, who had been warned in time and had been preparing the ground for some days, had more of less got the Emperor's agreement; when Abbé Ternisien was rich enough to do honour to his new situation and his elevation would cause no charge on the budget; and above all when the old Bishop of Lormières had been so violently stricken by illness.

'"Fortunately the second interview undid Abbé Ternisien, and brought you back to the surface. In a long conversation Monseigneur de Roquebrun had to expound the religious and political views of his protégé. He did it in such detail, and I may add with a frankness so unsubtle that thenceforward the Minister could have no doubt. They were suggesting that he should raise an enemy of the state to the episcopate. From that moment Monsieur Ternisien was finished; victory was on our side. The Government has had too much trouble with certain bishops, notably those of Moulins and Nîmes, to expose itself voluntarily to new religious adventures. Every affair with Rome, even the simplest, is involved with all sorts of difficulties.

'"As for you, my dear friend . . ."'

'But Vicar-General, that which touches you personally can in no way interest Monsieur de Castagnerte,' interrupted Abbé Mical, who was not pleased at these useless confidences.

Capdepont, submissive for the first time, threw the letter of Jérôme Bonnardot on the table and addressed the Vicomte: 'Well, sir,' he asked still quivering after he had read it, 'what do you think of this intrigue plotted against me?'

'I think that Monseigneur de Roquebrun, having by him a priest of the highest merit and the most perfect piety, had more than the right – he had the duty to help his rise to the episcopate.'

'What? Bishop Roquebrun knew, beyond doubt, that I had been distinguished by the Ministry, and that my name was among the first who should be elected – and his secret journey to Paris, and his efforts against my candidature, does all that seem natural to you?'

'It seems religious to me. Monseigneur de Roquebrun, imposing on himself the fatigue that killed him, wasn't thinking about you, sir, but about the Church.'

'That means, no doubt, that I don't think about it!' said Capdepont, advancing boldly towards Monsieur de Castagnerte.

The Vicomte did not give way an inch. 'You – you have enough to do to think of yourself,' he replied, in a sharp, contemptuous tone.

For a minute the two men, excited by such conflicting feelings, remained standing face to face, looking at each other like two enemies on the point of coming to blows.

Mical, horrified, slipped like an eel between them to separate them. 'Vicomte,' he said in a honeyed voice, 'it's late. And if you lose more time you won't find a priest in town to say your mass.'

Monsieur de Castagnerte could not help shrugging his shoulders. He went out.

'Well?' asked Abbé Lavernède, seeing him reappear in the sacristy of the cathedral.

'My dear friend,' answered the Vicomte, out of breath. 'St Paul has spoken of the folly of the cross. I have just seen the folly of the mitre.'

'Monsieur Capdepont?'

'Do you know that, but for my respect for his cloth, I would have struck this violent man across the face with my glove.'

'Tigrane has bitten you?'

'Not exactly, but he's shown his fangs.'

'And the mass?'

'You can say it now.'

Abbé Lavernède, who had already put on his alb and crossed the stole on his breast, assumed the black chasuble, and went to the high altar.

The cantors intoned the requiem.

At the same moment midday sounded from the great tower of St Irenaeus.

X

ROME

The sad news that was the talk of Lormières had flown to the four corners of the diocese, and busy priests arrived in crowds every day. Like a flock of black crows, parish priests, curates, chaplains fell upon the episcopal city, drawn from afar by the hope of prey. Not to speak of those who, in the hope of important diocesan appointments, pushed their way pitilessly, there was one on whom some censure had been inflicted, who came to protest against a former injustice; there was another who had been abandoned for twenty years on an inhospitable mountain crest, and hastened to beg for a change; another, grown grey in service, now painfully dragging himself on the stony roads of the Corbières, who came to ask for a pension.

Few were those who in formulating their requests and uttering their lamentations gave a passing thought to the memory of Monseigneur de Roquebrun. Certainly the late bishop had been good, indulgent, charitable and merciful to most of these pitiful petitioners, but he had made the unpardonable mistake of dying, and he was forgotten.

Moreover, into this oblivion entered an indefinable mixture of religion, resignation, profound wretchedness and shameful cowardice: they were afraid of Abbé Capdepont, whom each of them already envisaged as advancing with a mitre on his head and a crosier in his hand. Soon this man, whom they knew to be spiteful and vindictive, would have the honour and the livelihood of all of them in his control, and nearly all humbled themselves. It is easy to protest at the abasement of a priest when one does not know to what absolute power he is enslaved. The limitless authority of the bishops has produced the servility of the whole body of clergy. We may recall the haughty words pronounced by the Cardinal Archbishop of Rouen in the Senate on 11th March 1865: 'My clergy is a regiment; it has to march, and it marches.'

Abbé Rufin Capdepont, installed in the low room where we have just seen him, gave the most amiable of welcomes to this crowd of self-interested pilgrims. The violent eagerness of his ambition for the first time lent suppleness to this character, and to all of them he showed himself as obliging, lively and charming. To this old man he gave a hearty handshake; to this portly rural dean bouncing in his fat he made a joke about the austerity of penitence; to this smart, scented young curate he gave a gentle tap on the cheek, as if he were conferring confirmation before it was his office.

Besides, he took serious note of their requests, whatever they were, and finally sent them one after the other to Abbé Mical, his tool – who, hidden in an obscure corner, made them fall into the trap of a petition to the Government, and sent them away satisfied.

Nevertheless, although things were going well – in three days more than a hundred and fifty signatures had been collected – Abbé Capdepont seemed anxious. After the long march past of all those priests to whom, in his role as pretender to the episcopate he was obliged to address from time to time flattery or a caress, sometimes he fell into inexplicable discouragement. This weakness was the more surprising when he was informed every morning by Monsieur Jérôme Bonnardot of the state of his affairs in Paris, and had no reason to be alarmed.

What was going on in this mind, tempestuous as the sea when the slightest adverse wind begins to blow?

Abbé Mical understood nothing about this state, which was often near to being a fit, and he had come to ask himself if Rufin Capdepont was still the firm, impetuous, energetic man he had always known. What was the meaning of such prostration – when he was near to the goal of all the efforts of his life? the professor of moral theology was afraid that Capdepont had suddenly aged. Alas! he thought. Age brings with it this sort of physical and moral depression.

He anxiously followed him with his eyes, whether he walked to and fro in the big room to which they had retired as to an inviolable sanctuary, or whether he laid himself down in

80

an armchair, a prey to unknown discouragements, panting as if exhausted, with his mouth half open. 'He is ill!' he said to himself, and dared not question him.

One morning Abbé Capdepont, who had not opened his lips for more than two hours, rose abruptly from the chair on which he had been sitting and cried, with gestures of despair: 'No, Mical. No, Mical, I shan't be, I shall never be!'

'What? Do you mean you will never be bishop?'

Capdepont, with a frantic movement, seized an unsealed envelope from the papers piled up on the table, and took out a letter. 'Monsieur Bonnardot', he said, 'is a wise man. He asserts nothing of which he is not perfectly sure. Have you thought about this piece in his letter from Paris this morning? As for me, it struck me full in the breast like a dagger: "Here, I see no further obstacle to your nomination. If such a thing were to arise at the decisive moment it could come only from Rome. I have discovered that on that side, before leaving Lormières, Monseigneur de Roquebrun had taken active steps in favour of his protégé, and one of my friends, attached to the Apostolic Nunciature, told me that on the very day before his death the late bishop had seen the Nuncio and had presented Abbé Ternisien to him." That's how I shall be destroyed, Mical. It's by these hateful manoeuvres that Bishop Roquebrun will have succeeded in giving me the final blow.'

'Set your mind at rest, you're not dead yet. It's not to the Nunciature that the Government will look for its bishops. Let your nomination appear in the *Moniteur*, and Rome will yield.'

Rufin Capdepont continued his walk. 'For some days', he murmured, 'I've been troubled by gloomy presentiments. Last night I had a horrible dream. In this crushing nightmare I saw my own wreck. . . . These nocturnal fantasies shake you like poignant realities . . . I still tremble at it. . . . I was climbing a spiral staircase in the middle of a huge tower. At the top of this tower, exactly like that of St Irenaeus, all the symbols of the episcopate – the mitre, the crosier and the ring – shone in the light, and sparkled on a gold tray. I saw them distinctly – I went up, up, up. . . . Finally I got to the last step. Despair! It was inaccessible. Imagine, Mical, a cube of granite ten metres high, presenting a perfectly smooth surface to the eye. One would have to go to my village, Harros, among the great Pyrenees, to find a block like it. . . . How to attempt to climb this smooth, resistant mass? Where to set foot? Where to grip it with the hand? Cold sweat ran down my forehead and all over my face, and I had to turn my eyes from time to time to the dazzling mitre, to keep my courage from running out. . . . By dint of feeling the enormous rock in every direction, I found some slight cracks in it. Time does its work, even on granite. With my nails, made harder and sharper by rage, I detached some small fragments. . . . I shan't tell you, Mical, with what transports of joy I saw the stone crumble a little. Perhaps I should come to the end, and my heart swelled in my breast almost to suffocation.

'Finally, after several hours of hard, breath-taking work, all was ready for the assault. I surged up without hesitation. My feet and hands had suddenly taken on the appearance of real claws. I clasped the granite as closely as a reptile would, and could move easily. I remember my skin, stuck to the stone, felt its coolness, and being – as it were – one with it, I advanced slowly, surely towards the gold tray where lay all my desires, my fevers, my follies. What trouble, what efforts, what giddiness. But what a thrill in every fibre as I knew I was advancing. . . . The mitre and crosier, laid across each other, were radiant. I nearly touched them. Fascinated, dazzled, I took both my hands off to seize them. Oh, fearful catastrophe! I left my feet without support, and from the great tower of St Irenaeus I was hurled into space. . . . The blow I received when my head was dashed against the street woke me with a start. . . . I confess, Mical, that my forehead still aches and that since this morning I've found myself touching it from time to time to see if the skin hasn't been broken.'

Capdepont trembled all over, and his eyes were wild.

'That's childish,' interrupted the professor of moral theology. 'Let's be serious.'

'Serious! I was serious all the time. But you can't help the fact that Scripture shows us many dreams sent by God as warnings. Besides, doesn't the letter I got from Paris this morning make us face obstacles we had never thought of? . . .

Rome, that's the block of granite on the tower.'

'Taking it all in all,' said Mical, 'why should the Holy Father oppose your nomination – if indeed he is consulted, which I doubt? In spite of your publication about the Assembly of Clergy in 1682, I don't know that you've ever expressed opinions that aren't perfectly orthodox.'

'God forbid! . . . In attacking some of the privileges of the Roman pontiff, I proclaim loudly that I never intended the smallest attack on the Holy Church, my mother.'

'Well, then? . . . I hope it isn't your morals that they'll dare to attack.'

'I was chaste,' he said, with an emotional simplicity that left no doubt about this delicate and intimate side of his life.

'You see, then.'

XI

THE MINISTRY

Abbé Mical sat on a chair of coarse straw, one elbow on the table. He seemed in deep thought.

Capdepont pushed the chair by which he was standing nearer to the professor of moral theology, and sat down in his turn. 'My dear friend,' he said, taking Mical's hands in his own.

'But you have a temperature?' cried the latter, at the burning contact.

'My dear friend,' continued the Vicar-General, without letting himself be distracted from his worries, 'it's no good your trying to reassure me. I have the fears of a child, dreadful fears. And do you know where the terrors come from that crush me at this supreme moment when my fate is being decided? Henceforth it's no longer from Paris nor even from Rome – it's from on high!'

He lifted a finger, and pointed upwards.

'Mical,' he continued, 'in all this affair in which my life is engaged, I haven't sufficiently invoked the name of God. . . . I tremble. . . . Certainly, when the idea of rising to the episcopate first entered my mind, I was thinking only of the Church. It was only for the glory of the Church that I thought of climbing the ladder of the hierarchy. To become her support, it was so fine! I was still young, and though I had already experienced some of the movements of irresistible pride, the bitter strife of ambition hadn't yet stifled my enthusiasm or my simplicity. Happy time of my humble curacy at St Frument and at St Irenaeus! Alas, what a fall afterwards. . . . I wanted to become a bishop, and perhaps I shall be one day. But who can imagine my long martyrdom, and the humiliation to which I had to descend?

'Oh, there's something revolting in the humiliating situation that the civil laws have created for priests, whose intelligence and virtue give them the right to aspire to ecclesiastical dignities. Really, if one could go back to the election of bishops by the faithful, as it was piously practised in the early Church, why not turn the clergy in each diocese into an electoral body, and allow them to supply the vacancy of a see on the death of their former pastor? One would safeguard the dignity and honour of the priest in general, and that of the Sovereign Pontiff, who is now required to ratify every day, and often against his will, the choice imposed by governments? But no, after enslaving every institution to his will, the First Consul enslaved the Church as well. Bishops being able to become something like the prefects of consciences, he needed to keep the agents of power in his hand. It was a new instrument of power, *instrumentum regni.*

'So what had happened? The Church, having accepted or suffered the concordats, these iron chains that henceforth bind her to the policy of nations, has had to bear the consequence of all these events. She, made to soar in the blue sky above the heads of kings and peoples, has suffered hatred and contempt when she has been seen mixed up with the most wretched earthly interests. Since, instead of retaining her divine independence she has been enfeoffed to whatever prince it might be, wasn't it natural that in all our too frequent revolutions blind and hostile crowds should force on her a part of the responsibility?

'Ah, Mical,' he continued, with piercing sadness, 'how often did I feel drenched with bitter disgust while I was following this hazardous career of ambition, and went astray with the Thévenot family, afterwards attached to my work of intrigue! My first visit to the Ministry was a deeply painful stage. Certainly Monsieur Bonnardot, who did not desert me, left nothing undone to conceal from me the trials of my proceedings. But I had to sit in a waiting-room in the middle of twenty other petitioners, and there I measured the depth of my abjection. Imagine, chance had put me opposite a big mirror and there, if I just raised my head, I saw myself with my pitiful face, turning my hat in my hands, and not knowing how to hold myself. No words can depict the pain with which I looked at my soutane, my girdle, my bands. I was a priest, that is to say elected by God as dominator, pacifier, purifier of souls, and now I found myself on the worn bench of a waiting-room, hands on my knees, eyes dull, back bent, like a slave ready to receive the rod! Mical, I suffered this shame. . . .'

At this recollection he could not sit still; he got up and made further steps across the low room, gesticulating with a kind of madness.

'Frankly', said the professor of moral theology, 'I should have thought you more accustomed . . .'

'Accustomed!'

He stopped. Then fixing on his friend eyes that sometimes flashed, he said: 'Ah! Do you really think that I was frightened of all these men crammed in the Minister's waiting-room, or of the Minister himself? I was frightened of myself, fool that I was! It was that. Do you know what made me timid, constrained, embarrassed? It was my excessive strength. It happens to some men of my stamp. Moreover, the priestly character, which I never felt so strongly, was heavy on me with all the weight God has attached to it, and crushed me. . . . *Tu es sacerdos in aeternum*! A voice in me cried these terrible words. . . . Would that I had been a layman, that I might hold myself proudly on this bench of ignominy, but I was a priest. A priest ought never to be caught admitting ignoble motives, and my presence in this place was such an admission. A simple curate can present an attitude full of dignity if he is admitted to the presence of a bishop, a cardinal or the Sovereign Pontiff himself. With a minister he can only be low, if he is not insolent. It is strange, when my turn came to appear before the high functionary whom I had come to petition, I felt my breast full of wild passions. I was humble and yet I wanted to revolt. If the Minister, a formal, solemn personage, had said a tactless word to me, I should have exploded. . . . Why all this suppressed anger, you ask? Because outside the sacred hierarchy of the Church we should have no superiors. We aren't made to bow before laymen, but laymen are made to fall at our knees. It is to us that it has been said: "You are the salt of the earth."'

'With such ideas, when you left the Seminary you should have got yourself appointed parish priest at Harros, and have stayed there till the end of the world.'

'And how do you know that in the long, fevered years I

haven't several times been sorry not to have done so?'

Mical smiled slyly. 'Well,' he said, 'now you can satisfy yourself. As you're the highest authority in the diocese, why don't you appoint yourself curate in any village you care to choose?'

'You're joking, and you don't see that I'm suffering,' said Capdepont in a deep voice.

Mical left his chair and, seizing his friend's hands in an affectionate movement, he said' 'Come, that's enough exaggeration. It's the moment to see things clearly and not to be troubled by fantasies. Ah, they are very right to blame you for not being practical! Perhaps you have genius, but certainly you often lack common sense.'

'Let's leave it.'

'What's it about, after all? You're afraid that if the Emperor appoints you Bishop of Lormières, the Sovereign Pontiff, warned against you, may refuse to sanction it. I'm not without some apprehension of such a thing myself, but I don't exaggerate. If Monseigneur de Roquebrun had enough credit with the Vatican to get his complaints heard there, remember that in Rome they're not in a position to show too much hostility to the decrees of our government. The Pope lives by the protection of the French Army.'

'But who knows what the hatred of Monseigneur de Roquebrun may not have invented to destroy me. Have you forgotten that in the conference chamber, before the assembled diocese, this man – totally unworthy of the position of bishop, which he had usurped by low intrigues – had the extraordinary audacity to lift his hands against me, and murmur the formulas of exorcism.'

'I can still see that scene. He compared you to Lucifer, Prince of Darkness. . . . But don't let's cry in the wilderness, it's a waste of time.'

'Then don't pronounce the name Roquebrun!' said Capdepont, whose savage spirit, which for a short time had been tamed by discouragement, was again aroused.

Abbé Mical was silent for a few minutes. Then, suddenly bringing down his big hands on his friend the Vicar-General's thin shoulders, he shook him.

'What are you thinking of?' asked the latter, fixing his light, phosphorescent eyes on those of Mical, who was scared and bowed his head.

All the same the professor of moral theology kept his right hand over his mouth, and still thought in silence.

'For pity's sake!' murmured Capdepont, in an almost begging voice.

'I think', said Mical slowly, 'that whatever reports have been sent to Rome against you, there's a way to nullify them.'

'A way?' The hideously contracted face of the capitular Vicar-General cleared up.

'It would be enough to attempt in Rome what we have succeeded in doing in Paris.'

'A petition?'

'No, but a long application to the Pope, in which your perfect orthodoxy and your unshakeable attachment to the Holy See are established.'

'And who will guarantee these opinions? At bottom they are mine. But haven't I appeared to betray them by my approach in Paris to a government determined in its search for Gallicans?'

'First of all, we'll have numerous quotations from your works, then signatures.'

'Signatures? . . . Most of the priests summoned to Lormières have gone back to their parishes. Must we call them again?'

'What need is there for all those people? Let the chapter answer for you. Eleven signatures – I don't want any more.'

'The chapter!' cried Capdepont. 'Ah, Mical, sometimes you have good ideas . . .'

'In France our cathedral chapters are confined to such insignificant privileges that in effect they are only a useless luxury round the bishop. It's another matter in Rome. They've kept all the prestige of ancient ecclesiastical foundations, and you feel the weight . . .'

'Certainly. But are you sure of the chapter of Lormières? I'm afraid of three or four being reluctant.'

'The canons will obey the Dean, and old Clamouse, in spite of his weakness the other day, is on our side. Besides, I'm going to employ my strategy to conquer any resistance that reveals itself.'

Light as a squirrel, he pounced on his hat.

Capdepont looked at Mical with amazement and curiosity.

'News this evening!' said the professor of moral theology, reaching the door.

Capdepont made two steps towards him; then, suddenly stopping he said: 'My friend, just now I was regretting – in this great matter, my elevation to the episcopate – to have neglected the name of God. If, at the moment of these last efforts, we were to kneel down. . . .' His voice trembled.

Mical was moved, and allowed himself to be led by the hand to the table. Above the accumulated papers a fine ivory crucifix held out yellowed arms.

They knelt on the bare flagstones.

XII

THE VOICE OF THE CRUCIFIX

Next morning Abbé Capdepont left the Great Seminary, where he was still staying, at an early hour, and hastened to shut himself up alone in the big room of the bishop's office. Several letters awaited him on a corner of the table, which had been cleared of useless papers by an unknown hand. The Vicar-General vigorously spread the pile of correspondence about and his eye sparkled as it rested on a small, square envelope almost entirely covered with large handwriting.

Capdepont read eagerly . . . his face brightened, and his lips began to smile . . . he turned the page and continued . . . suddenly all his face darkened, and his forehead, which had been smooth, wrinkled from one temple to the other. 'It's defeat!' he said.

He crumpled the letter in his long bony fingers. His teeth ground together. He fell on to a chair as if collapsing under a blow by which he had been violently struck.

The letter, whose first lines had the privilege of making the terrible Canon smile, and whose conclusion almost prostrated him, was from Baron Thévenot. Sent post-haste from Paris about the affair which for years he had made his own, the former deputy gave a faithful account of his proceedings.

He had managed to interest his old friend Dupin senior, now senator and attorney-general at the court of appeal, in the candidature of Abbé Capdepont. He did not doubt that the very favourable intervention of the author of the *Handbook of Ecclesiastical Law* would deal the last blow to the Emperor's hesitation.

It was unfortunately certain that, despite the insistence of the Empress, always firmly attached to the success of her protégé, the Emperor, worked on by General de Roquebrun, who had inherited his brother's rancour, hesitated between

Capdepont and Abbé Ternisien. Abbé Ternisien had a large fortune, a consideration which was important in the eyes of the Government. A rich bishop does much good to religion and to the State.

The decree, anyway, had been drawn up. The question was what name figured in it.

As for Abbé Ternisien, whom he would have much liked to see in order to sound him out, he had not been able to meet him in Paris. After having spent some time over the embalming of his protector, he had disappeared. One imagined that he had gone to Arras, where the de Roquebrun family waited to bury, no doubt with ceremony, the body of the former Bishop of Lormières.

The activities of Abbé Ternisien ought to be watched, and he would watch them attentively.

This Ternisien, who was placing himself in the way of his ambition, threw Capdepont into the cruel alternatives of discouragement and despair. Was it really possible that they dared to set up against him a man hardly forty years old, quite unknown in the Church, to which he had never given the least service by word or writing? What was this young cleric, fresh from the Franciscan convent at Tivoli, without works or real merit, compared with him, who for twenty years had never passed a day without speaking or writing; who had presented to the altar several generations of distinguished and virtuous priests; who had re-edited the complete works of St Thomas Aquinas, published several treatises of which one, *de auctoritate*, was a classic in more than thirty seminaries; commented on the admirable *Soliloquies* of St Augustine; who at the moment was collecting information to clear up an obscure point of history: the relations between Pope Sixtus V and King Philip II of Spain?

Sometimes, puffed up by the feeling of incontestable superiority, Capdepont came to the point of pitying his rival. 'Come!' he said, with a contemptuous movement of his shoulders. 'We're not made to fall foul of each other on the same road.'

He could be in no doubt, however: it was Monseigneur de Roquebrun's former secretary who had risen up against him.

Capdepont remained motionless, his eye fixed on his agent

Thévenot's letter. The paper of this unlucky letter was falling to pieces between his clenched hands.

What should he try to do?

He reflected. . . .

He raised his arms abruptly, and let them fall on the table. The papers rustled. Some bundles came undone and were scattered on the floor. A frightful anger was gathering, and if, as Seneca says 'there is in man a god and a beast tied together', it could be said that in this madman the tiger, glimpsed by his former fellow pupils, had broken its chain and begun to roar.

As was his habit, when he was troubled by stormy thoughts, Rufin Capdepont began to walk without noticing. He went from one wall to another, his brows knit, his rough hair bristling like a mane, now gesticulating, now speaking. The commentator on the *Soliloquies* of St Augustine (also an impetuous character, but subdued by charity – *caritate*, as he himself said) abandoned himself in his turn to the bitter sweetness of giving free rein to his thoughts in solitude.

In his frantic walk he recited to himself in detail the long torture of all his life.

It was about twenty years ago that the evil had begun. He enjoyed the memory of his time in Paris. Then everything seemed fine to him; the future spread out vast and radiant before him. Besides, he was so young! Ah, his youth! Suddenly – by a leap in his thought, he came to Monseigneur de Roquebrun. He stopped short. His irreconcilable enemy emerged from the shadow; he touched him.

Capdepont halted for a moment, he did not dare make a step or pronounce a word. The excess of his hatred made him immovable. His eyes shone like burning coals, turned on the imaginary figure he seemed to see poised in front of him. By an effort he unstuck his feet, which seemed glued to the flagstones; his tongue that was fixed freed itself at the same time.

In a sort of mad hallucination the Canon, out of his mind, passed all bounds. He had just accused Monsieur Jérôme Bonnardot of negligence, the Thévenot family of stupidity, the Archbishop of Paris – from whom he had wrung a promise to serve him – of egoism, all his friends of imbecility or

92

cowardice, but what did he not say of Monseigneur de Roquebrun?

For him the late Bishop of Lormières was the real culprit, the sole culprit. After having addressed the most hateful abuse to him, he went so far as to refuse the poor dead man the quality of simple probity. Having found a deficit of three thousand francs in the diocesan funds, a deficit amply justified by Monseigneur de Roquebrun's abundant charities, he accused him of stealing money, as he had accused him of stealing the mitre.

Is man really so made that passions can absorb him to this extent? Alas, yes, man is so made. A weaker Rufin Capdepont might have been moderate; the energetic Rufin Capdepont, absolute, born for domination, had to show himself excessive by the very law of his blood and nerves. For some characters, whatever their social position, there is a sort of ineluctable ferocity.

Suddenly there was a sound; a voice had spoken in the silence of the vast room. The Vicar-General, who at this minute was tearing Abbé Ternisien to pieces – that stumbling-block which Bishop Roquebrun had thrown him from his tomb – was seized by a sort of sudden fear, and became still, in the middle of his fiery speech.

Where did this sound, that he had distinctly perceived, come from?

He listened.

Rufin Capdepont trembled in all his limbs; neither his long studies nor his contact with the world had terminated superstition in this obstinate character. Priest and peasant, he always believed in the marvellous. God had intervened. God judged him. . . . Perhaps God threatened him!

He went with reverence to the table and, kneeling on both knees before the Divine Crucified, as he had done the day before with Mical, he composed himself and prayed.

93

XIII

THE CHAPTER OF ST IRENAEUS

It was in this posture so natural to a priest that the chapter of St Irenaeus, guided by Abbé Mical, surprised Rufin Capdepont. The Dean, Clamouse, advanced and touched the shoulder of his kneeling colleague with the tip of his trembling fingers. Capdepont turned quickly at this contact: his face was pale and one could discern on his burning cheeks the traces of recent tears. Prayer, that sacred weapon within man's reach, had it opened his heart? Had he wept?

He rose and greeted the members of the chapter.

'Capitular Vicar-General,' said the Archpriest Clamouse, 'at the moment when the canons of the Cathedral, with all the clergy of the diocese, were rejoicing in the hope of your speedy enthronement in the see of Lormières, a rumour has been spread abroad which troubles and worries us. In his anxiety to push his secretary into the episcopate, Monseigneur de Roquebrun, on the very day before his death, is said to have denounced you to the Sovereign Pontiff as tainted with heterodox opinions. The chapter of St Irenaeus cannot be insensible to the calumny which touches it in its most illustrious member. Knowing the purity of your doctrine, and having long since read your works, we have drawn up the following protestation, which we now address to the Vatican.'

Then the Archpriest, with as much energy and solemnity as his age allowed, read six long pages in which a number of extracts from the Superior's books were collected. The whole had been put together in that easy and barbarous Latin, unknown to the Rome of the Caesars, which the Rome of the popes has made popular in all the world.

Abbé Capdepont listened seriously, without turning a hair. 'Gentlemen,' he replied, 'I can only show myself profoundly touched by the kindness and delicacy of the attempts you are making for my rehabilitation with the Holy Father. I thank you. I especially thank you, Archpriest Clamouse, who have always been the first to take alarm when there was any question of my defence, and who incessantly strove for me against my enemies. I do not know what will be the fate of this important document which is going to Rome, but I cannot doubt that if it is placed under the Pope's eyes it will nullify the false imputations of Bishop Roquebrun. I have written a preface to Bossuet's *Déclaration*. But what does that mean? Because, following the example of the great Bishop of Meaux, I formulated certain reserves in favour of our ancient French ecclesiastical law, is it to be inferred that I was in rebellion against the Sovereign Pontiff? Pius IX, more sorely tried than any of his predecessors has been, knows only too well to what constraints we have been obliged by the civil laws that have strangled the Church, to pause over the aspersions that have been cast at me. . . . Gentlemen, you whose eyes and hearts have always constantly turned towards Rome, that heavenly light – *lumen in caelo* – do you need my confession? Oppressed by the concordats I'm Gallican, being unable to be ultramontane. Have you understood? Let the government which has usurped the privilege of naming the bishops – *naming* you understand? – set its choice on Rufin Capdepont, and Rufin Capdepont will prove in a striking manner that he loves Rome and hates Paris!'

'Long live Pius IX!' cried Abbé Mical, raising an arm towards a portrait of the Pope that hung on the wall.

'Long live Pius IX!' repeated Capdepont with enthusiasm.

'Long live Pius IX!' said all the canons in chorus.

A sharp knock sounded on the door.

Abbé Mical went to open it.

Oh, surprise! On the threshold appeared pale, worn out, covered with dust, the former private secretary of Monseigneur de Roquebrun, Abbé Ternisien.

'What, you here! You, a stranger to this diocese, you dare!' And Rufin Capdepont sprang up to block his entry.

'Capitular Vicar-General,' said Abbé Ternisien with great gentleness, 'I have just come from Paris. I have brought the body of Monseigneur de Roquebrun.'

'Was there no room for this corpse in the cemetery at Arras?'

95

'Don't you know, sir, that for centuries the Bishops of Lormières have been buried in the cathedral?'

'Bishop Roquebrun in the vaults of St Irenaeus!'

'An ancient custom.'

'And you counted on me to proceed with this burial?'

'On you, sir, yes . . . but in default of you, on the city of Lormières, which will know how to give its late bishop a worthy funeral.'

'A scandal?'

'It is you who have desired it. . . . Already the whole populace is going to the station, and the women of the Paper-Mills, who have not forgotten their benefactor, are strewing the route that the procession will pass with branches of cypress.'

'The procession! . . . Of what procession are you speaking, pray?' asked Capdepont in ironical amazement.

'That at the head of which your title of capitular vicar-general makes it your duty to walk.'

'My duty! You dare speak of my duty, sir? I have never forsaken it, and would to God Bishop Roquebrun had shown himself always servant to his! The diocese owes nothing to this man, who filled it with ruin and disaster. Wasn't it he who, under the pretext of reforming our liturgy, completely upset it? Wasn't he always pitiless to the poor curates in the country? Wasn't it he who quite lately turned the most distinguished and respected priests out of the Great Seminary? Finally wasn't it he who, contrary to the manifest wish of all the diocese to see me one day occupy the see of Lormières, went off secretly to Paris with the intention of ruining my candidature and making it fail?'

'Reassure yourself, sir. Your affairs are not so desperate as you seem to think.'

'And what do you know about it?'

'If you have been alarmed because my name has been put forward, banish all anxiety. I shall never be a bishop.'

The frankness of this quite unexpected avowal disconcerted Capdepont. Thinking of Machiavelli, he feared his credulity was being abused.

'Italian!' he murmured between his teeth.

He continued in a louder tone, staring at Abbé Ternisien with his big eyes wide open.

'It is none the less true that during your stay in Paris you saw the Nuncio, you saw the Minister, perhaps the Emperor . . .'

'I had met the Apostolic Nuncio twelve years ago in Rome.'

'And the Minister?'

'Monseigneur de Roquebrun was in such a state of health that I felt it my duty to accompany him everywhere.'

'Even to the Tuileries?'

'Even to the Tuileries, when his affairs called him there.'

'His affairs!' cried Abbé Capdepont with rising anger. 'You mean your own, no doubt?'

'Your snares are obvious, sir. I see them, and shall not fall into them. As it is not my habit to lose my temper, I say only what I wish to say.'

These words, pronounced with icy self-control, lashed Rufin Capdepont like a whip. 'You hear, gentlemen, you hear him!' he cried, at the height of exasperation. 'Did I not tell you that Abbé Ternisien had long meditated on that book, *The Prince*? He knows how to be silent and how to speak with purpose. Is not all the art of diplomacy there? What a bishop we shall have in him if they heed the recommendation of his protector. . . .'

Abbé Ternisien very calmly made a step forward.

'It is understood, then, Vicar-General, that you refuse to proceed with the solemn funeral of Monseigneur de Roquebrun?'

'I refuse. If you wish to bury this dead man that you bring from Paris, you are free to do so, but do not expect any of us to be present at the ceremony.'

'Very well. This afternoon at four o'clock I'll put on my surplice and go alone to receive the body at the station. The crowd of faithful people will recompense me for the desertion of treacherous clergy.'

He bowed, and went out.

The clergy who had been present in bewilderment at this shocking scene, whispered among themselves.

Suddenly Abbé Mical hurried to the door, but Capdepont, on the watch, seized his arm roughly. 'Whither away so fast?'

he asked.

'I'm running to tell Abbé Ternisien that you yourself will receive the body.'

'I forbid you. It will be treachery on your part.'

'In that case – you wish to destroy yourself absolutely?'

'Yes!'

This savage cry threw another ray of light on the character of this priest, in whom hatred went even deeper than ambition.

XIV

LAVERNÈDE AND TERNISIEN

Leaving the diocesan offices, Abbé Ternisien took the empty rue St Frumence and went towards the Hôtel Castagnerte. There he was expected not only by the Vicomte, who was very impatient, but by General de Roquebrun, who had come from Paris to be present as chief mourner at his late brother's funeral.

Shaken by the violent resolution of Capdepont, Abbé Ternisien walked slowly despite the urgency. When he arrived, what should he say to Monsieur de Castagnerte? Above all, what should he say to General de Roquebrun? Nothing hurts and humiliates a priest so much as to make certain admissions to laymen. In his eyes it would do great harm to religion if the faithful were to be initiated into the private strife of the sanctuary. God sees the shame; that is enough.

Abbé Ternisien was almost at the door of the Hôtel Castagnerte and still did not know what line to take. In short, it would not have cost him much to reveal to the Vicomte the situation that the intractable Vicar-General had created; Monsieur de Castagnerte was a religious man, and well informed of old about the character of Rufin Capdepont. But Ternisien could not resign himself to telling anything of what had occurred to the brother of his former protector.

If Monsieur de Roquebrun, an old soldier full of petulance in spite of his sixty-eight years, learned that the capitular Vicar-General of the diocese refused to be present at the ceremony for which he himself had come to Lormières, and that all the clergy of the town were scared by his example and meant to imitate his abstention, of what fury would he not be capable? Certainly he would rush to Capdepont and demand an explanation of his conduct. What a conflict there would be between these two men: the priest exasperated by hatred, the soldier by grief! In any case Ternisien had no doubt that if he and Monsieur de Castagnerte by their entreaties could persuade the General simply to scorn the insulting absence of the Vicar-General and clergy of Lormières, he would certainly telegraph to Paris and inform the Ministry, and perhaps the Tuileries, of the facts that he must take to heart so deeply. Then what would happen?

Abbé Ternisien trembled. A thought, like a flash of lightning, illumined the darkness of his mind: perhaps the terrible Rufin Capdepont was about to commit the huge error that would throw him down from the episcopate to which he was so near? Did not God permit this sort of savage blindness, in order to make the unworthiness of this ambitious man burst forth in public? Instead of trying to check the man and his uncontrolled fury, one ought on the contrary to leave him to his unbridled passions, and if possible to irritate his pride still further, to destroy him more surely.

Exalted by the feeling that he had a great service to render to the Church in letting Capdepont compromise himself to his heart's desire, Ternisien felt the mass of scruples that had assailed him fall from him one by one. . . . Yes, he would speak: he would tell all to the Vicomte and the General.

The heavy gateway of the Hôtel Castagnerte was in front of Monseigneur de Roquebrun's former secretary. He put a hand on the massive copper knocker, but withdrew it quickly.

Poor Abbé Ternisien, always undecided like all weak people! Alas, the situation was very serious, and his fear returned. He retreated a few steps. . . . For a minute he stood still. . . . Abruptly he left the rue St Frumence and entered the little rue des Bernardins. It was in the middle of this narrow street that Abbé Lavernède lived, and Ternisien, hard pressed, and sinking under his burden, was going to ask for advice and support before undertaking anything.

'Well, at what time is the removal of the body?' asked the prison chaplain on his appearance.

'At four o'clock . . . we will do it alone.'

'Alone! What do you mean?'

Abbé Ternisien related his interview with Rufin Capdepont.

'Good!' cried Abbé Lavernède, whose eyes sparkled with

100

joy. 'Here's a man who doesn't deceive you, and though I'm disgusted at the attitude that he thinks fit to adopt on this solemn occasion, at least I'm obliged to him for his frankness. But where was Mical – always there as this madman's keeper?'

'Mical was there, also the Archpriest Clamouse, and all the chapter of St Irenaeus.'

'And no one intervened – before the coffin of our sainted bishop?'

'No one dared.'

Lavernède shook Ternisien's hands vigorously. 'My dear friend,' he said, 'let us hope Capdepont will persevere in his appalling obstinacy. As God has not permitted Abbé Mical to save him this time, it is clear that he is abandoning him. The hour draws near when this rebel, this *Prince of Darkness* as Monseigneur de Roquebrun called him in the conference chamber, will in his turn be thrown down from Heaven. No, he won't be Bishop of Lormières!'

'Alas! I told you this morning, when I left Paris the decree was sent for signature to the Emperor.'

'Are you sure that the name of Capdepont was written in it?'

'They thought so, at the Nunciature.'

'All the more reason to catch the ball at the rebound; and to give our enemy – God's enemy – the chance to ruin himself irrevocably. Didn't you once tell me that Monseigneur de Roquebrun, certain that no kindness would tame the Superior of the Great Seminary, counted on the violence of his unbridled nature to rid the Church of him?'

'That's true. But my deep affection always contrived to hold Monseigneur back, and to avoid a conflict.'

'Perhaps you were wrong.'

'Forgive me, dear friend. The very thought of a conflict between two priests makes me shiver. Think of what I had to suffer when it was a question of Capdepont and Monseigneur de Roquebrun. . . . A moment ago, in the offices of the episcopate, I stood up to the Vicar-General, and I assure you that the vehemence of his words did not in the least intimidate me. . . . But do you know what happened inside me? While my lips were quick to retort, I felt my heart as big as a mountain and wanted to cry.'

'Poor child!' murmured Abbé Lavernède, moved to the depths of his feelings. And he hugged Abbé Ternisien with affection.

'I don't know what to decide,' stammered the latter, trying to dodge the emotion that was overwhelming him. 'At one moment, going along the rue St Frumence, I felt great energy arising in me. Since Rufin Capdepont offered war, I decided to accept it, and to mobilize all those who could fight for justice with me – General de Roquebrun, the Vicomte de Castagnerte, you yourself – then I was appalled by the consequences of the strife. Perhaps we shall succeed in making Capdepont fall into the snare he has set himself. But at what cost would this success be gained! We would have to let Lormières and the Catholic world into quarrels it is better they should know nothing about.'

'What does it matter?'

'What does it matter? . . . Have you thought, Lavernède, of the confusion a public scandal could bring to sincerely pious lay folk, and on the contrary of the joy it would arouse in those who profit by the least excuse to attack religion? The former would bow their heads sadly, the latter would lift up theirs radiantly, crying: "See how the priests live among themselves." For be sure, once the battle is engaged, Capdepont won't retreat. If his obstinacy were to cause the most serious damage to the clerical character with which we are all invested, nothing could hold back this madman. He will go to the very limit of his ferocious insanity, and in this frightful internal laceration any consideration of the clergy in general or his own dignity will be overcome.'

'In all this, my dear Ternisien, you seem to me to be more concerned with Capdepont than with the Church.'

'But it is just because I'm concerned with the Church that I'm afraid to come to blows with this man, who's a priest like you and me.'

'It's a duty, however.'

'And if it were a sin?'

'Then,' went on Lavernède, getting more and more excited, 'instead of seizing on the wing the chance you're given of letting Rufin Capdepont publicly denounce himself as unworthy of the episcopate, you prefer to see him chosen and appointed as Bishop of Lormières? Take care, Ternisien. You are at the point of committing one of those weaknesses for which a life of tears and repentance could not atone. What? An ambitious man covets and is going to obtain the see of Lormières, distinguished by so many holy prelates – and God, who doesn't wish to abandon this diocese to the wicked man, rouses you, and you refuse to become the instrument of His wrath and His justice! Again, take care! . . . If you are afraid of a conflict with Capdepont, be more afraid of the responsibility which will henceforward weigh upon you. On whom will God lay the blame for all the evil that Capdepont cannot fail to let loose in the Church, if not on him who, having the task to cut off the evil at its root, had not the courage to try? . . . Make no mistake, Ternisien. Capdepont, Bishop of Lormières, is Satan turning the diocese upside-down, subduing our poor clergy, already so lacking in resolution, self-respect and daring, to all the caprices of his pride, stamping each priest with the brand of the most shameful servitude. Ah! He spoke to the poor curates of the tyranny of Monseigneur de Roquebrun! I feel my whole being revolted at the thought of what his would be. So much for the beginnings of Capdepont's career. But what may not happen? What will be the limit of his ravages? If you think Capdepont will be satisfied for long with the little diocese of Lormières, one of those least in view in the Catholic world, you little know him. Soon you'll hear that he's set his heart on the *pallium* of an archbishop. Imagine the Prince of Darkness in purple, and thus disguised whispering in the Church the spirit of revolt and sedition . . .'

'But Rome would never . . .'

'Rome? Our mountaineer of Harros has outwitted Paris. He'll outwit Rome too. Certainly I haven't forgotten that in the Vatican they have men gifted with marvellous acuteness, but – forgive a vulgar word – Capdepont will diddle them. The Vicar-General's long, thin body doesn't seem to you made for cutting capers like an acrobat, and his stiff, bony hands don't seem the right thing for conjuring tricks. Undeceive yourself! If Tigrane has the ferocity of that feline whose name has stuck to him, he has also the suppleness. Besides, why not admit to yourself that this man has a prodigious intelligence? That God, whose designs are inscrutable, has put a divine brain into his hard, obstinate skull? You remember that one day, in the presence of Monseigneur de Roquebrun and of the chapter of St Irenaeus, Abbé Mical dared to call Capdepont a "great man"? The chapter – the Dean, Clamouse, first of all – burst out laughing, Monseigneur himself smiled slyly. I alone remained serious, thinking that if friendship had pushed Mical to exaggeration, Capdepont was none the less a man quite out of the common. I'm sure no cleric in France surpasses him in knowledge. And then his eloquence – abundant, full of colour and vigour. What depth, and sometimes what soaring transports! Are they not like flights of an archangel's wings? During the twelve years that I lived side by side with this dominating personality, the feeling of this, and of his unconquerable pride stamped on the smallest of his discourses, often spoiled for me his learned dissertations on Scripture, and his brilliant and rapid digressions across the pages of ecclesiastical history. Why not admit it? In spite of the small, infernal flame that I distinctly saw flicker above his forehead, how often was I subdued by the despotism of his enchanting eloquence and the incomparable charm of his mind?'

'Lavernède, don't be afraid. The Holy Father hasn't got only clever men round him, he has God.'

'I know.'

'And when Capdepont goes to Rome . . .'

'Take care that he doesn't. You are foolhardy, for if he goes they will listen to him, and all will be lost. Are you simple enough to think that, once named bishop in Paris, Rufin Capdepont will take to Rome the harsh and violent character with which we identify him here? Calmed down by the realization of his dearest wishes, Capdepont will leave behind in Lormières and in the Great Seminary – discreet witnesses – all his errors and outbursts, and in the Vatican he will appear gentle, affectionate and simple as a child. He will soon have given all the guarantees of respect and obedience. Why should he get irritated now? What reason could he have to give those savage cries against God and man that were drawn from him by the intolerable humbleness of his condition? Isn't he a bishop, a prince of the Holy Catholic Church?'

'Enough, Lavernède, enough! Please! You've brought me to the edge of an abyss – and I've lost my balance.'

'You're a priest – that is, a man of sacrifice. Instead of being cast down, the sight of danger should strengthen you.'

'Why did I leave my solitude in Tivoli?'

'God had need of you in Lormières and called you here,' answered the prison chaplain.

Electrified by these words, Abbé Ternisien rose from the chair on which he had sat collapsed. 'My friend,' he said in a firmer tone, 'Monseigneur de Roquebrun, who appreciated you too late, and was beginning to love you. . . . What must I do?'

'It's quite simple. While I warn the heads of all the communities in the town to robe, and go to the cathedral, you will go down to the Quarter of the Paper-Mills, where your name is better known than mine, and you'll invite the workmen and their wives and children to the ceremony.'

'So I'm to leave General de Roquebrun in ignorance of my conversation with Capdepont?'

'In complete ignorance. We shouldn't allow the enemy of the Church to go back on his mad decision, and a visit of the General at the diocesan offices would give him an outlet to safety. Would the Vicar-General dare refuse to Monsieur de Roquebrun what he has refused you? I doubt it, for Mical would certainly intervene this time. As Capdepont has unsheathed the sword, let him run himself through with it, and die!'

'But Monsieur de Roquebrun will have to be informed?'

'Certainly, but when there's no more time to risk any step towards Capdepont. You understand. . . . The General will be present at the removal of the body. He will notice – if necessary we will make him notice – the absence of the capitular Vicar-General and the mass defection of all the parish clergy of the city. Naturally Monsieur de Roquebrun will resent this rudeness. Once we have returned from the station with the body of our bishop, the people of the Quarter of the Paper-Mills will murmur, and cry "Down with Capdepont!" Monsieur de Castagnerte will arrange this. As for me, while you arrange a mortuary chapel on the ground floor of the bishop's palace, I shall take the angry General to the telegraph office, and I'll compose a telegram accordingly, which the Minister will read tonight, and perhaps the Emperor. Besides, I

105

shall see that this telegram is in the *Echo de Lormières* tomorrow morning, and the day after tomorrow in the *Universel de Toulouse*. We'll see if the candidature of Rufin Capdepont recovers from this blow!'

'My God! My God!' murmured Ternisien in terror.

'Go to the Quarter of the Paper-Mills, remind the good folk by the Arbouse what Monseigneur de Roquebrun was to them. Above all, don't worry about the General. I shall come out with you, and go straight to the Hôtel de Castagnerte.' Then, looking fixedly at poor Ternisien, who was trembling: 'My friend,' he said, 'before God and man I accept absolute responsibility for what you and I are doing.'

The last words were pronounced with piercing sincerity.

Abbé Ternisien bowed his head. Lavernède took him by the arm and led him down the stairs.

XV

MICAL

The two priests had not made thirty steps in the rue des Bernardins when they came face to face with Abbé Mical, coming out of the rue St Frumence.

'Here you are, at last, Monsieur Ternisien,' said the professor of moral theology. He took a large red check handkerchief and wiped his sweaty face. 'What stifling heat!' he went on. 'Lavernède, may we go into your house for a moment?'

'You must understand, Mical,' answered the prison chaplain crossly, 'that on a day like this neither Monsieur Ternisien nor I have any time to spare. You can explain yourself at once.'

'You think, perhaps, that I'm involved in the folly . . . I mean the caprices of Capdepont?'

'So you admit the man is mad?'

'Let us be agreed, my friend, and not take fire like gunpowder.'

While exchanging these words with animation, they had gone back to Lavernède's little house. Mical opened the door with the ease of a frequent visitor and hopped into the hall; the others followed with a bad grace. They went into a room on the ground floor.

'Well?' asked the prison chaplain. 'What do you want?'

At this point-blank question the little eyes of Mical blazed, but he repressed a violent desire to lose his temper.

'My word, Lavernède, you are questioning me exactly as if I were appearing in front of a tribunal. Do you mean to judge me, perhaps? If I were able to laugh today when all the city is in mourning, I should be much amused at your words and your airs of grandeur.'

'Don't restrain yourself, Mical. Laugh. That won't surprise Abbé Ternisien or me,' answered the prison chaplain who, guessing that his plans against Capdepont were going to be thwarted, tried to aggravate the situation and make a conflict inevitable.

The professor of moral theology was as cunning as a fox. He scented a snare, and addressed the former secretary of Monseigneur de Roquebrun.

'Sir, I have come from the capitular Vicar-General to express his regret at having given you a reception this morning so unworthy of you and of himself. The multiplicity of his business and the ceaseless work to which he has had to condemn himself for some days has put the Vicar-General into such a state of nervous debility that there are moments when everything tires, irritates, exasperates him. Through ill fortune you came to the bishop's palace at one of these bad moments. Besides, one must admit, that certain words attributed to Monseigneur de Roquebrun, and basely repeated in Lormières and the diocese, have further excited Abbé Capdepont. But the calm, which he never completely loses, has come back to that great mind, and the Vicar-General asks me to give you not only his apologies, but at the same time to assure you that he will preside at the convoy of the body of Monseigneur de Roquebrun at the head of all the parish clergy of this cathedral city. Nevertheless, he asks, in view of the crushing heat, that the ceremony may not take place till six o'clock. There is now daylight until nine.'

The good and simple Ternisien, seeing every difficulty removed and all conflict rendered impossible, could not refrain from pressing Mical's hand in his own. He said, with emotion: 'Please thank the capitular Vicar-General and tell him how touched I am by a change of heart that does honour to his character as a priest.'

The professor of moral theology looked furtively at the prison chaplain. His monkey-like face sparkled with malice, the whole of him – eyes, nose, lips and chin – laughed with a cruel laugh. 'You don't seem pleased, my good Lavernède?' he hissed, taking a large pinch of snuff to conceal the too insulting irony of his features.

'Yes, I should have preferred that Capdepont had had the courage to push things to their conclusion, rather than to inflict on himself this pitiful come-down.'

'But the Vicar-General never seriously intended to refuse to Monseigneur de Roquebrun after his death the homage that he never refused him during his lifetime.'

'The Vicar-General! . . . The Vicar-General! . . .'

'He is, my friend, he is! . . . Besides, in the past of Abbé Capdepont there is nothing . . .'

'Do not let us stir up the past!' interrupted Lavernède animatedly. 'And if your commission – which you could as easily have carried out in the street – is done. . . .'

Mical did not notice the gesture of the prison chaplain, who showed him the door.

'Perhaps you planned to exploit the absence of the Vicar-General?' He threw out these words as if at random.

'I defy him to persist in his resolution.'

'Don't defy him, my poor Lavernède. He's stronger than you, you know.'

'Yes, certainly he is stronger than I am, if strength in a priest consists in an absolute contempt for his duty.'

'Take care! If he became Bishop of Lormières he might very well not give you back your chair of sacred rhetoric.'

'And who tells you, sir, that I should consent to receive it at his hands?'

'And if he took away your chaplaincy of the prisons? What would you do about your invalid old mother?'

'Wretch!' cried Lavernède. 'You dare come to my house to threaten me!'

Abbé Ternisien quickly interposed: 'Gentlemen, gentlemen, calm yourselves!'

'My dear Lavernède, how excited you get! How excited you get!' said Mical, taking a step towards the door.

'I don't think you get excited enough,' said Lavernède.

The professor of moral theology stood still, and turning to his opponent his little, mean, grimacing, treacherous face, he said: 'One day, perhaps I shall get angry too, but that day is not yet come.'

And he escaped.

XVI

THE CONVOY

From five o'clock, at the moment when the sun in a glory of great red clouds inclined towards the Hautes Corbières, whose high crests shone, all the bells of the town awoke with a start. One by one the bells of the various parishes answered the great bell of St Irenaeus which began to toll, and one after another the little bells of the communities sounded in this grand and solemn concert of bronze.

Lormières, drowned in the rays of the setting sun, was full of rumbling, of which the nearby mountains from minute to minute sent back the echo. Sometimes the noise was such that one seemed to distinguish crashes of thunder amid the peal of bells hurled from every rope and clapper.

Moreover, the heat was still extreme, and huge brown masses, like heavy chains of granite, rose and obscured the East, and slowly closing against each other heavily covered the vast fields of the sky.

The procession towards the cathedral began only at about six o'clock. The Capuchins, headed by their provincial, were the first to leave their convent; then came the Barnabites, then the Dominicans, then the Marists, then the Jesuits from the College of St Stanislas Kotska. Each of the priests held a lighted candle in his hand.

But the sight became quite original when the parishes of the city came from every side with the multicoloured banners of the lay corporations, crosses as tall as trees and banners raised on long coloured poles. The religious, men and women of different orders, had slipped by silently; one just caught the murmur of their prayers. Ah! but now it was quite another thing! The lay folk gossiped and laughed and shouted to each other. In all the South of France religion is a spectacle.

This noisy crowd, here and there among which groaned

some devout women, at last arrived in compact masses, and by all the roads, in front of the porch of St Irenaeus.

'God damn me! Let me pass or Christ will fall down!' cried the crucifer of the Blue Penitents, worn out under his giant crucifix.

In five minutes the huge basilica was inundated, from the door to the rails of the high altar. The clergy, among whom were Lavernède and Ternisien, had managed to detach themselves from the crowd and went to the sacristy to join the officiant, whom they were to follow.

Abbé Capdepont, as if he had some hidden reason to wish to delay the ceremony, had not yet put on rochet and cope. On the high platform of the sacristy he was talking to Mical and several canons. The conversation seemed to be exceedingly animated.

It's probably about me, thought Lavernède.

He was no longer in doubt when Rufin Capdepont turned and looked at him: the anger that filled his heart shone in his eyes.

Abbé Ternisien, always on the watch, advanced. 'Capitular Vicar-General,' he said, 'General de Roquebrun has just entered the cathedral – if you care to give the signal for departure . . .'

Capdepont did not answer. Mical gave him the rochet and the stole, then the black cope. He put everything on, fuming with ill temper.

'Come, gentlemen,' said Mical.

Abbé Capdepont appeared in the nave of St Irenaeus surrounded by numerous clergy. His long, yellow, bony face now had a surprising look of calm and serenity. He raised a hand with a proud gesture, and the procession moved.

They stopped at the station just long enough to place the coffin on the hearse, decorated with ample black drapery enriched with escutcheons of the late bishop's arms. After this torrid day the threatening sky continued to grow darker, and now that the bells were silent it was no longer possible to mistake the hollow rumbling of thunder in the distance. The sound did not come from the Corbières, but from far into the Pyrenees, whose peaks from time to time lit up like beacons.

Moreover, it must be admitted that Rufin Capdepont, on

whom this ceremony was imposed by fate, was anxious to see the end of it, and it was not the prospect of a storm that caused him to make haste. Placed last, at the end of the procession, he walked with great strides, gloomy and serious, his deep, light eyes fixed on the hearse which, on its progress down the streets, women, old men and children vied with each other in covering with flowers. Every fresh wreath falling on the coffin stirred up in the evil soul of the capitular Vicar-General an infinite ferment of anger and vengeance. All the time one word escaped his pallid lips: 'March! March!'

Finally his sufferings came to an end: after detours that seemed to him interminable, they arrived in the cathedral square. 'Silence!' he cried.

The *De Profundis*, chanted all the way from the station, ceased.

Rufin Capdepont, pressed by Abbé Mical, who signed to him, went up the steps of the bishop's palace. From that eminence, in a few able words he thanked the people of Lormières for the devotion they had always shown to their bishops, and invited them to the funeral of Monseigneur de Roquebrun on the following day.

'But sir, the funeral cannot take place tomorrow,' interrupted Lavernède.

'And why not, if you please?'

'Remember, Vicar-General,' replied Ternisien, 'that no work has yet been undertaken in the vaults of St Irenaeus. The architect will need a day or two.'

'I have spoken!' replied the intractable Capdepont.

Suddenly night fell. An enormous cloud, detached like a block from the great chains of mountains that rose against the blue of the sky, rolled in front of the sun and cut off its last rays. The frightened crowd, fancying they already felt rain on their backs, dispersed in all directions.

General de Roquebrun himself went away on the arm of the Vicomte de Castagnerte. Soon no one was left in the square of St Irenaeus but the robed priests. They were waiting in cruel anxiety. What were they waiting for? No one knew anything. They could only guess from the severe, almost tragic attitude of Capdepont, and the frightened air of his acolyte Mical, that some event was in preparation.

112

The Abbés Ternisien and Lavernède, with looks of anguish, furtively drew close to the hearse, their eyes fixed on the coffin of him whom they had loved so much. Did they fear it would be taken away from them? All sorts of mad ideas went through their minds – they began to wonder why their legs could no longer support them. . . .

What was going to happen?

XVII

POPE FORMOSUS

Meanwhile Rufin Capdepont, stiff and immobile on the free-stone steps, raised an arm towards the undertaker's men. 'Take down the coffin, and bring it here,' he said.

The men obeyed.

The clergy, wild with curiosity, invaded the court of the bishop's palace, and Mical cautiously shut the gate.

The coffin had been placed on the gravel. Ternisien and Lavernède, followed by some religious, among others by the Provincial of the Capuchins, a little old man with a white beard, made a living fence round the dead bishop. All were full of strange fears.

'Are you afraid they'll steal this corpse from you?' laughed Capdepont, pushing with his big hand five or six Barnabites who had imprudently placed themselves in front of him. Then, with a haughty step, walking round the coffin to enlarge the narrow circle of the religious, 'There must be room for the priests of the diocese,' he said.

Some rays of sunlight filtering through the heavy clouds that filled the sky, fell on the pall of Monseigneur de Roquebrun and died.

The great clock of St Irenaeus struck eight.

'Gentlemen,' went on the Vicar-General, turning to the small group of canons of the cathedral which the Dean, old Clamouse, had just joined. 'They have brought the corpse of Bishop Roquebrun from Paris and we are asked to bury it in the vaults of our basilica, hitherto reserved to saints.'

'Since Monseigneur de la Guinaudie, the chapter hasn't refused this honour to any of our bishops dead at Lormières,' interrupted Lavernède.

'It is possible that you may soon have to account for your conduct before the diocesan court. Meanwhile, sir, I ask you

114

not to interrupt.'

'I shall interrupt every time that you choose to let your hatred speak, instead of justice.'

'My hatred?'

'Yes. In refusing the vaults of St Irenaeus to the prelate lying in this coffin, you are pursuing vengeance.'

'And if that were so!' cried Rufin Capdepont, exasperated by this opposition, and perhaps counting too much on his prestige and authority.

The Principal of the Capuchins went up to him. 'If it were so, Vicar-General,' he said, in a voice trembling with age, 'if it were, I, an old man of eighty-four, older than the Archpriest Clamouse here present, should not hesitate to condemn you. Vengeance is always hateful on the part of a priest, and in the circumstances in which we are assembled, it would be infamous.'

'You do not know, Father, that Bishop Roquebrun, on a day of fearful anger, compared me to the Prince of Darkness, to Lucifer, struck down by God.'

'And have not you fomented sedition, like the rebel angel?'

'I think, Father Provincial . . .'

'Our Divine Master has said: "Who takes the sword, shall perish by the word" – *Qui gladio . . .*'

'Sir!'

The old religious bowed and went back into the line.

Abbé Ternisien could not restrain his tears. 'Monseigneur was a saint,' he repeated wildly. 'Monseigneur was a saint! . . . Gentlemen of the chapter, I beg you . . . Monsieur Clamouse, you who knew Monseigneur de Roquebrun and received so many proofs of his goodness. . . . All of you, gentlemen, curés of Lormières. . . .'

A glacial silence met this heart-breaking prayer.

Abbé Ternisien, who had bowed to the parish clergy, pulled himself up. He hurriedly dried his eyes and went up to Capdepont. 'Sir,' he said, 'the body of Monseigneur de Roquebrun cannot lie any longer on the stones of this court. Allow it to be placed in the salon of the bishop's palace. I will at once arrange to turn that room into a mortuary chapel.'

It seemed that he was unheard.

The poor young priest was mad with grief. Suddenly with a

movement of extreme devotion he threw himself on the coffin of his dead master, clasping it with both hands and trying to move it. 'Oh God! Oh God, do a miracle!' he said. . . . Raised from the earth, it fell back with a dull thud.

The diocesan priests looked on stupidly, too cowardly to intervene.

Abbé Lavernède and several Marists hastened to help Ternisien, but Rufin Capdepont stopped them with a gesture. 'Gentlemen,' he said, 'we must not think of introducing this coffin into the bishop's palace. Monsieur de Roquebrun has left numerous debts, and to indemnify his creditors I was obliged to ask the competent authorities to seal all the doors of the palace. The late Bishop of Lormières was always prodigal of other people's money. Have we not ascertained a large deficit in the clerical pension funds. . . ?'

'Sir,' retorted Ternisien, 'will you kindly recollect that Monseigneur de Roquebrun spent his entire fortune, about five hundred thousand francs, in founding an almshouse for the aged, that he created a shelter for young invalids, and that, all over the diocese, he helped more than three hundred families . . .'

'As for the mortuary chapel of which you speak, there could be no question of it. Would it be proper to expose to the sight of the faithful a face made hideous by apoplexy? "A bishop should preach even after his death," St Gregory the Great has said. I ask you all what the convulsed features of Bishop Roquebrun could preach to the people, except the violence, anger and all the evil passions of which his soul was full.'

'You lie, sir, you lie!' cried Ternisien, transported with indignation. He lent over the coffin and quickly pushed back the six hooks that held the lid; and he opened it.

The priests, struck by the sight of their bishop, stepped back in fright.

Capdepont himself retreated a few steps.

Monseigneur de Roquebrun, laid on a bed of satin, shot with silver and set off with violet ornaments, seemed to be sleeping. His face, calm and reposed, breathed an angelic sweetness. His cheeks, a little puffed, were soft, and had the faintly yellow matt surface of ivory. A white mitre was on his head, and his

116

right arm was gently disposed along the golden crosier placed at his side. His pectoral cross fell on a spotless white chasuble. The shining fringe of a rich stole fell on his feet, whose tips in the middle of the folds of his alb showed two small silk slippers hemmed with a black border.

The sight was grand and touching.

'Don't be afraid, gentlemen,' said Lavernède with biting irony. 'He's dead, he's quite dead.'

The clergy, as if stupefied, came near and looked eagerly.

The Vicar-General did not move. His proud head held high, and a bitter and sardonic smile on his lips, his burning eyes went round the crowd, sometimes rested on the wan face of the dead bishop, sometimes on the canons of the cathedral chapter whispering together, among whom the fat Abbé Turlot was fidgeting.

But Mical seemed preoccupied; the lines on his forehead betrayed grave anxiety. Suddenly, pushing his keen face forward, he muttered a few words in a low voice to Rufin Capdepont who, lost in black thoughts, came back to a sense of the situation.

'Gentlemen of the chapter,' he said, 'in my capacity as capitular Vicar-General, I could decide the question which has been occupying you and have the body of this dead bishop buried in the town cemetery tomorrow. But I thought it right to consult you before taking a decision of such importance. For ten years, like myself, you have been able to judge Monsieur de Roquebrun in action, and you know if his stormy episcopate, so fatal to this diocese and to the Church, deserves the honour we are urged to give him. Remember, my dear colleagues . . .'

'Remember, gentlemen,' interrupted Lavernède, 'that when Monseigneur de Roquebrun arrived in Lormières our city lacked hospitals altogether, and that thanks to his inexhaustible charity it has three today . . .'

'Remember,' went on Capdepont, his voice turgid with anger.

'Remember', interrupted the bold prison chaplain, 'that thanks to Monseigneur de Roquebrun two hundred sisters of charity, here and there among our mountains, care for the sick, teach the children, bring up orphans . . .'

117

'Monsieur Abbé Lavernède, I am your hierarchical superior. Again I order you to be silent. Remember that I have the power to censure you and, if I wish to go so far, to suspend you and interdict you.'

'Interdict me! . . . I'm known in Lormières and in all the diocese, sir, and I defy you to touch my sacerdotal character.'

'Take care!'

'I'm not afraid. I shall never be afraid of you.'

'I summon you to appear tomorrow before the diocesan court.'

'I shall appear, and God have pity on you and me!'

A long murmur of disapproval rose from among the parish clergy.

'Monsieur Lavernède,' interrupted Clamouse. 'The chapter blames the violence with which you have just spoken to one of its members. It asks you for calm and moderation.'

'And I ask everyone here – even you, Archpriest – to remember the sacred respect due to the dead.'

Some of the religious, and a few rare secular priests who had no doubt been scandalized, detached themselves from the different groups and seemed about to retreat.

'One moment, gentlemen,' said Rufin Capdepont, halting them. Then returning to his haughty attitude he said, in a solemn voice: 'The coffin of this bishop open in front of us reminds me of one of the most sinister episodes in our ecclesiastical history. This really dreadful event is the story of Pope Formosus exhumed at the orders of Stephen VI and cited to appear before a council. Stephen accused Formosus of having usurped the Sovereign Pontificate, and the council was of his opinion, for they severed the head of the corpse, and cut off the finger which wore the pastoral ring, and then threw it into the Tiber. . . . I, who know by what worldly intrigues Abbé de Roquebrun, Canon of Arras, managed to invade the episcopate, have I not the right to set myself up as judge, and when they dare to ask me to place his remains in the vaults of the cathedral, to place them in a pauper's grave? Has not this man deserved this disgrace?'

'No, no!' cried Abbé Ternisien. 'Gentlemen of the chapter, you are being deceived, you are being misled . . . I swear . . .'

'If you attempt to take away this coffin, to bring it to the

118

town cemetery,' said Lavenède, planting himself in front of Capdepont, 'we shall tear it from your hands and bury it in the vaults of St Irenaeus.'

'Who are "we"?' asked the Vicar-General with shameless contempt.

'I myself, the Abbé Ternisien, these religious here, all the priests of the diocese who haven't yet submitted to your yoke.'

'A fine army to resist my legitimate authority!'

'You speak of an army? Beware! The people of Lormières haven't yet forgotten Monseigneur de Roquebrun.'

'The people of Lormières?'

'They hate you. One word from Abbé Ternisien would be enough to have you cut to pieces.'

'A riot?'

'And didn't a riot break out on the day when Stephen VI threw Pope Formosus into the Tiber? As it pleased you to recall to us the passions of a barbarous century, you should have carried your story further and not omitted to tell us that the people of Rome, infuriated at Stephen's cruelty, arose against that unworthy pontiff, seized him, threw him into a cell, and strangled him there without pity.'

'Horrible, horrible!' murmured the Provincial of the Capuchins.

Capdepont did not answer. Fascinated for a moment by the really magnificent sight of a bishop asleep in all the pomp of his pontifical ornaments, while Lavernède was speaking he went quietly up to the coffin to see things from nearer. . . . My God! How beautiful the mitre was! He looked at it lengthily, his eyes alarmingly dilated. And the crosier, how splendid! How well he would lean on this curved rod! How well this rod would grace his dignified, masterly bearing! He was dazzled by the big amethyst set in the massive gold of the pastoral ring. He stood still. Ah, to wear this shining ring on his finger! He could not restrain himself, and with an abrupt movement he disengaged the heavy folds of his black cope, held out his burning hand, eager as the claw of a vulture, and dropped it on the icy hand of the dead man.

'Heavens!' cried Abbé Ternisien. Throwing himself on Capdepont, he pushed him off. The lamb had the strength of a bull.

'Well, well!' stammered the Vicar-General with an appalling calm. 'What is all this about?'

'Wretch, it's that you have just committed the most horrible crime – sacrilege!' replied Abbé Lavernède, rushing towards him and threatening him with a raised arm.

'I? I?' he said in astonishment.

It was clear that Capdepont had no consciousness of the crime of which he was reproached. When passion goes deep enough, it makes people quite irresponsible. Capdepont, in prey of an ambitious monomania, as alienists would say, had a second of real madness.

Meanwhile the court of the bishop's palace was in a state of tumult. Abbé Mical, the Archpriest Clamouse and members of the chapter distraught with horror had surrounded the Vicar-General and all spoke to him together.

'Take him away, gentlemen. Take him away!' cried the Provincial of the Capuchins in the midst of the noise. 'This man isn't a priest, he's a demon. I've seen the fires of Hell blazing in his eyes.'

Rufin Capdepont still struggled, gesticulating and shouting. Mical, Clamouse and the canons, with whom nearly all the parochial clergy joined, had the upper hand, and pulled him away.

XVIII

THE REGULAR ORDERS

This appalling scene was followed by a long moment of stupefaction.

Abbé Lavernède was the first to recover from the shock. He bent down, and while Ternisien was still motionless he quietly replaced the lid on Monseigneur de Roquebrun's coffin and closed it. Was not Capdepont capable of escaping from the arms that held him, and of suddenly reappearing?

'Gentlemen, let us pray,' said the Provincial of the Capuchins in a heart-broken voice. At once all knees bent.

Abbé Lavernède, to whom the moment of calm induced by prayer brought back in full strength the memory of what had passed before his eyes, suddenly rose to his feet. Without knowing why, all the priests imitated him and rose.

'Gentlemen,' said the prison chaplain, 'it is of great importance to the Church that information should reach the highest level about the really criminal conduct of Monsieur Rufin Capdepont. I shall run and tell the General de Roquebrun, so that he may at once send a telegram to Paris.'

'What? You wish the laity to know what has just happened here?' asked the Provincial of the Capuchins. The old man trembled.

'We must give this affair the greatest possible publicity,' answered Lavernède.

'Stop, sir. At this moment you are speaking like a priest who has lost the spirit of his vocation.'

'But Reverend Father, if we wish to prevent the nomination of Monsieur Capdepont as Bishop of Lormières, we have the strict duty to denounce him to the world.'

'God has cursed the world, and we have only one strict duty towards it, to save it.'

'Ah, no!' cried the prison chaplain, pushing aside the

religious round him, to make his way to the gate of the courtyard. 'No, no. In spite of you I shall deliver the Church from the danger with which she is threatened.'

He detached himself violently. He was just taking off when Ternisien seized his two hands. 'My friend,' he said, in an imploring voice, 'stay with us. Please, not a word of all this to General de Roquebrun. Are you sure that at his age the news of the insult to his dead brother, and to all his family, would not kill him?'

'Then do you want this insult to be inflicted publicly? At ten o'clock tomorrow, Capdepont, after finally persuading the chapter, will publicly refuse to bury our bishop in the vaults of St Irenaeus.'

'He won't dare,' everyone murmured.

'He won't dare? He who, under the cover of history, asked us to judge Monseigneur de Roquebrun, to sever his head, to cut off his right hand, and to throw his body into the Arbouse after dishonouring it by these mutilations!'

'Calm down, Monsieur Lavernède, in the name of your priestly character, calm down!' interrupted the Prior of the Dominicans, a grave and much respected person.

'Listen, all of you. Have we no arms to defend our beloved bishop against the attacks of Rufin Capdepont? No. Are we resolved to make this corpse the empty tabernacle of a soul so pure, so made of love and charity, duly respected? Yes. Is this not true? Why, then, in the lamentable extremity to which we are reduced should we hesitate to have recourse to the civil power which, with one word, can put an end to the most odious scandal there ever was? You're afraid the blow will be too much for the General? Very good, he will know nothing. But allow me at once to send a telegram to Paris on my own responsibility. This evening the Minister will be informed, and he will have all the time he needs to give orders to Capdepont for the ceremony tomorrow.'

'Subject to the possibility of exhuming him when circumstances allow, it would be better for the Church that Monseigneur de Roquebrun should be buried in the cemetery of this town than to inform the lay authority of the unhappy divisions that have broken out here,' said the Prior of the Dominicans. 'Monsieur Lavernède, a priest is not free. First of all, he owes loyalty to that body to which ordination irrevocably bound him. Monsieur Capdepont is to blame, very much to blame. But what do we gain by divulging his crime?'

'We gain the knowledge of having accomplished that sacred thing called duty.'

'The laity are our enemies.'

'I know no enemy but Evil.'

'Evil isn't among the priests – it's among men. The clergy is the holy ark placed above the agitations of the world. We must leave it on the height where the hands of God have placed it.'

'Why forbid me to throw down the pride of Rufin Capdepont?' cried Lavernède in exasperation. 'Did not God blast the most beautiful of His angels?'

'Then wait until God's arm is seen in the heavens.'

At the same moment a red flash illuminated the court of the bishop's palace, dazzled all eyes, and thunder crashed. The old cathedral, all of whose echoes were awakened, trembled on its granite base. Twenty terrified priests fell on their knees, others bowed their heads. Only the Prior of the Dominicans remained upright in his place. The candle which he held in his hand palely shone on his rigid profile. It was as if one of the statues had suddenly come down from its niche in St Irenaeus.

'Monsieur Lavernède, God, whom you invoked, has heard you,' said the white-robed friar slowly. Then he too fell on his knees.

The storm, whose distant rumblings had been perceived about five o'clock, had advanced slowly behind thick clouds, and now threatened to break over the town. From all points of the horizon the monstrous masses, some dense black, others transparent here and there and fringed with silver, were detached by the repeated claps of thunder and moved heavily over Lormières. They met in the vast space above the high tower of St Irenaeus. The drifting clouds stopped there, clashed against each other, and formed a chain of frowning mountains, something like a hundred Himalayas accumulated in the infinite fields of the sky.

To the left of these Cyclopean heaps, where a poet's eye might have seen the formidable ramparts of the city of God, the moon had kept a little place to shine in. From this look-out post, continually narrowing, some rays fell on the houses of

Lormières, whence not the smallest sound arose. Other rays glanced on the faces of the clouds, illuminated the deep gorges here, the fearful precipices there, and farther away seemed to shine on an army in helms of steel, with shimmering breastplates, and sharp, glittering swords.

A new flash furrowed through this moving mass. The sky changed its aspect. No more splendid army, no more precipices with picturesque crags or caves with shining stalactites. It was henceforth chaos, with a yawning chasm in the middle. In this black gulf the moon had disappeared; the night was frightful. Suddenly drops of rain, large and round as small coins, fell on the hands of the priests in the court of the bishop's palace.

Without a word the Provincial of the Capuchins, whose bare feet were little protected by his open sandals, took off his serge cloak and spread it on the coffin of Monseigneur de Roquebrun. In a minute ten others, with the same pious purpose, took off their cloaks.

Abbé Ternisien sprang to the great door of the bishop's palace and shook it with all his might. 'Impossible,' he murmured in despair.

He ran to a small isolated building belonging to the administration of the diocese, and knocked repeatedly in vain.

'Gentlemen,' he said, coming back, 'the cathedral is not shut until nine o'clock, and it is not yet nine. Let us carry Monseigneur to the cathedral.'

The rain increased, putting out the lighted candles in the priests' hands.

'Quick!' said Lavernède in an authoritative voice.

Fifty hands fumbled in the darkness, and lifted the Bishop's coffin by a common effort.

'Forward!' said Abbé Ternisien.

One candle still burned, that of the Prior of the Dominicans. This severe friar headed the column. The funeral procession arrived without hindrance beneath the porch of St Irenaeus.

Abbé Ternisien leapt to the door and raised the heavy iron latch. Although the regular hour had not yet struck, the cathedral was closed.

'Heavens!' said the poor young priest, ready to faint.

124

The bearers laid down their burden on the very threshold of the cathedral in the most sheltered place.

'It's infamous!' the Prior of the Dominicans could not help saying.

'It's devilish!' said the Provincial of the Capuchins.

'Gentlemen,' cried Lavernède, 'I shall have the keys of the cathedral, or I'll go down to the Quarter of the Paper-Mills and have the doors broken open.'

He was surrounded. 'Leave me alone!' he cried, struggling. 'Leave me alone!'

'Do you want to bring back Monsieur Capdepont?' asked the Prior of the Dominicans.

'Are you afraid of him?'

'It's useless anyway to provoke new scandals.'

'All the same, the body of our bishop cannot remain exposed to the rain. You cannot wish this, Father Prior, you whom Monseigneur de Roquebrun distinguished among all the religious of Lormières, and who as often felt the effect of his fatherly affection!'

The dry, angular face of the Dominican turned pale under the light of the candles, now relit. The austere friar was overcome by the memory of the benefits he had received.

'What are you complaining of, Monsieur Lavernède?' he said. 'You, a priest of this unhappy diocese, you ought to be glad that the coffin of your bishop suffers the affront of this terrible storm. For my part I wish that the rain falling in torrents may invade this last retreat, and that we may be reduced to mounting guard under the porch, up to our knees in water.'

'I don't understand you, Father Prior.'

'Suppose the civil power, which cares so little for the interests of our holy religion, names Capdepont Bishop of Lormières, do you think the Holy Father will ever appoint a priest who has been unafraid of outraging the dead?'

'So, Father Prior, you mean to write to Rome?' said Lavernède, breathless with sudden joy.

'I mean to tell my General what I have just seen. He will also know all the details of this horrible evening we are passing. And if later there is good reason to proceed to canonical

125

investigations about Monsieur Capdepont, a copy of my letter will be placed by my superiors in the apostolic archives.'

'On my side, I shall act like you, Father Prior,' the Provincial of the Capuchins made haste to add.

'Oh, my Reverend Fathers, my Reverend Fathers!' stammered Lavernède with emotion. Then, running through the groups, 'Where is Father Trézel? Where is Father Trézel?' he repeated. 'He must write to Rome too.'

Father Trézel, director of the College of St Stanislas Kotska, had left long before.

'Oh, the Jesuits, always so clever!' said Lavernède with a laugh. 'Capdepont may become a bishop, and they have followed Capdepont. It's their doctrine. One must manage to live in peace with the powers that be. . . . My God!'

He went across to the coffin . . . he looked attentively at the cloaks that covered it, lightly raising them one by one as if counting them . . . he spread them again on the oak boards. . . . His attitude showed a wild and bitter grief. The others looked at him in surprise, mingled with fear.

'Poor Monseigneur de Roquebrun!' sighed Ternisien.

Abbé Lavernède raised towards the former private secretary eyes brilliant with little tears. The rage of powerlessness by which his soul was wrung had made these tears burst out. 'My friend,' he said finally, 'do not cry any more. Monseigneur is going to enter into his cathedral.'

And before any hand could restrain him, he dashed into the darkness, into a storm like a whirlwind, and was lost to view.

XIX

THE ARCHPRIEST'S WHIST

The cathedral vomited water out through all its gargoyles, and veritable cascades were discharged from the roof-tops over the flooded town.

Abbé Lavernède, at a run, crossed St Irenaeus' square, which was plashing in water. He arrived at the corner of the rue St Frumence. A lamp, hanging from an iron bracket, shed its dim and trembling light on a tall black house with pointed windows. This house, fragment still standing of an ancient Benedictine abbey, had a gloomy appearance.

The prison chaplain stopped in front of a low door, studded with great nails with shining heads, and he raised a heavy knocker cut into facets. There was a strident noise and the door opened a crack.

'Heavens! How wet you are, Monsieur Lavernède!' a woman exclaimed.

'Are the keys of the cathedral here?'

'I think so. The sacristan brings them every evening.'

The servant raised a bit of yellow wax, once in service at St Irenaeus and now finishing its existence as a light in the Archpriest's kitchen, and she looked behind the massive door.

'Oh, it's extraordinary!' she said. 'They're not hanging on the nail as usual.'

Lavernède himself looked.

'Jésu-Maria! Monsieur L'Abbé, don't keep this rain on you. You'll be ill.'

'Is Monsieur Clamouse in his sitting-room?'

'Certainly! He's playing cards with these gentlemen.'

The prison chaplain was horror-struck. What! The former Bishop of Lormières was enduring the storm, and more than a hundred religious, some of them very old, were receiving the rain on their backs – and two paces away from the cathedral porch, open to the winds and downpour, other priests were playing cards!

He went down a long passage, prey to every kind of thought of rebellion, hatred and contempt. Without first knocking, he opened the wide glass door of the sitting-room. Four heads, profoundly concentrated under the green lampshades, looked up quickly. They were the Archpriest, Professor Turlot, and the first and second vicars of St Irenaeus.

'My dear Lavernède,' said Monsieur Clamouse, whose parchment face shone with unspeakable content. 'A slam, a superb slam! . . . We'll talk in a minute. Pay attention, Turlot, pay attention!'

'I'm very sorry, Archpriest, to interrupt your whist at such a critical moment, but . . .'

'No nonsense, Turlot,' went on Clamouse, who had not heard the prison chaplain. 'Pique!' . . .

'But Monsieur Lavernède, you're as wet as a water-rat,' said the first vicar with an air of pity; and he forgot to throw his card on the table.

'And what's that got to do with you?' interjected the Archpriest acidly. . . . 'Play, sir.'

The first vicar's card fell on the carpet.

Abbé Lavernède went up to Monsieur Clamouse. 'Archpriest,' he said, in a voice trembling with indignation, 'there's a terrible storm. The rain is falling on the coffin of Monseigneur de Roquebrun.'

Monsieur Clamouse allowed a movement of impatience to escape him.

'After all, a coffin only contains a dead man, and he doesn't care if he receives rain or sunshine – pique again!'

'This dead man was your bishop.'

'But he isn't any longer. . . . Pique!'

'That, no doubt, is why you dare to defy him. I remember you had less courage in the conference chamber on the day of the ordination.'

With a stiff little gesture the Archpriest gathered all his cards together in his right hand. For once he could not go on with the game. A distraction, and he lost his famous slam.

'Monsieur Lavernède, you respect nothing,' he said, with

the most comical seriousness. 'Evidently you know nothing of the game of whist! . . . As I've got to listen to you, speak! What do you want?'

'I want the keys of the cathedral.'

'And it's for the keys that you're making all this fuss? Am I stopping you from taking them? Take them, and leave us in peace – hold on, Turlot!'

'The keys aren't hanging in their place, Archpriest.'

'Then the sacristan hasn't brought them yet – come on, Turlot!'

'But why precisely this evening, when the cathedral could offer a resting-place for Monseigneur de Roquebrun's coffin, has the sacristan closed the doors before the proper time, for it is not yet nine o'clock? Was it not you, Archpriest, who gave this order?'

'I!' said Monsieur Clamouse, who this time turned purple with shock and let his cards drop on the carpet.

'Then I beg your pardon.'

'How, sir,' said the angry old man, 'could you have thought me capable of that?'

Lavernède was touched, and seized his hands with marked respect. 'Archpriest,' he said, 'of course you are not capable of committing the atrocious cruelty of Rufin Capdepont on your dead bishop. No, despite some yielding to the Vicar-General, a yielding explained and perhaps excused by the inflexibility of the hierarchy, you could not give the lie to your long life as a priest, which Monseigneur de Roquebrun – as he lately told you – so often quoted to us as an example. I implore you to forgive the suspicion which for a moment crossed my mind. . . . I'm quite confused today.'

Just as he had done once in the conference chamber, when against his will he had been put at the head of a sort of conspiracy, Monsieur Clamouse wept. 'My dear Lavernède,' he mumbled, 'go and claim the keys of St Irenaeus from the sacristan in my name, and if you don't find him, and I'll sack him for failing in his duty, have the coffin of our holy bishop brought here. My house will be honoured to serve as a mortuary chapel.'

The two vicars, on whose young, free hearts Capdepont had

not yet set his brand, rose from their seats and went on either side of the Archpriest. 'Well done, Archpriest, well done!' they said.

Only Abbé Turlot remained silent, motionless, his big, pasty face hidden behind his cards, spread in a fan.

'Archpriest,' said the prison chaplain, 'you offer shelter to the wandering corpse of your bishop. God sees your heart and you'll obtain mercy, even if for a minute you listened to the voice of the Demon. But it isn't this house, it is the cathedral that must be turned into a mortuary chapel. I'll run to the sacristan's house.'

As Lavernède had just opened the glass door of the sitting-room, the first vicar of St Irenaeus stopped him.

'Sir, don't go to the sacristan's, it's useless. The cathedral keys are here.'

'Here?'

'Yes.'

'In my house?' said Clamouse in amazement.

'I am truly grieved that Abbé Turlot, by his inexplicable silence, compels me to denounce him. It is he who closed the doors of the cathedral and put the keys in his pocket. I saw it all.'

'Why was that?' cried old Clamouse, indignantly addressing the professor of Holy Scripture. 'And you allowed us to wrangle like this?'

'Archpriest, do you want us to finish this game of whist or not?' asked Turlot, who pretended to attach no importance to what was going on.

Lavernède no longer felt any restraint. In Turlot he had neither age nor position to respect. With a frantic gesture he snatched the cards from his hand and scattered them over the room. 'The game is over, sir, it's over,' he said. Then devouring him with eyes blazing with rage he said: 'The keys! The keys!'

At this attack, Turlot stood up in turn. 'When I closed the cathedral,' he stuttered, 'I was obeying the orders of the capitular Vicar-General. It is therefore to Monsieur Capdepont that I shall return the keys of St Irenaeus, not to you.' He seized his hat, which he had left on a chair, and tried to escape.

But Lavernède shut the sitting-room door again. He resolutely planted himself opposite his adversary. His face, already sad, had become tragic. 'I shall not allow you to escape, sir!' he said.

'Do you mean to do me violence?'

'If in the struggle which you are provoking I happen to forget that we are both priests, it will be you who wished it.'

Abbé Turlot, terrified, and white beneath his usual pallor, stumbled towards the Archpriest. 'Archpriest,' he said, 'as I can no longer guard safely what Monsieur Capdepont has confided to me, I am putting it in your hands. I don't think anyone will have the audacity to snatch it from you. If you are tempted to yield to the behests of Monsieur Lavernède, remember that the capitular Vicar-General himself ordered that the cathedral should be closed to avoid the scandals that might be provoked there tonight, and that he alone has the right to have the doors opened when he thinks fit.'

'But I'm the curé of St Irenaeus!' ventured old Clamouse, receiving the keys from the hands of Turlot.

'Indeed, the Archpriest is master in his own church,' intervened the two vicars.

'There is only one master the length and breadth of the diocese, and it is the capitular Vicar-General.'

'Nevertheless, canon law . . .' Clamouse ventured to insist.

'The capitular Vicar-General – no one doubts – will soon be raised to the episcopate of Lormières, and as he has a good memory he will remember those who disobeyed him.'

'So you think seriously, my dear Turlot, that it would be to disoblige the Vicar-General if . . .'

'I think, Archpriest, that you would incur all his anger – and his anger is terrible, you know.'

Poor old Clamouse, in the grip of every sort of fear, sank into his armchair and sat there crushed and speechless, looking with a dull eye at the bunch of keys that clinked in his fingers.

Abbé Lavernède, certain to triumph over all obstacles, whatever they were, looked on at this miserable scene with an air both calm and sad. With his arms crossed over his breast, he looked at the pitiful expression of the Archpriest and could not help feeling a sort of bitter disgust. This priest, brave and firm in the face of so much feebleness and shame and cowardice, felt wounded in his priestly character, in that which his vocation preserved of divine. It was no longer a question of

131

Monseigneur de Roquebrun, but of Clamouse and Turlot, and the heart-rending spectacle that his two colleagues offered was crushing. What power Rufin Capdepont had! To what degree could Rufin Capdepont degrade those whom ordination should have made 'Brave as David, Wise as Solomon'. He thought of the Prince of Darkness and the legions he had drawn with him into the abyss.

However, an end must be made of it. The sight of such debasement in a high dignitary of the Church was too painful to the prison chaplain. He vigorously pushed away Turlot, who was leaning over Clamouse and speaking to him in a low voice. Then, looking at the old man who was bent in two by dejection, he said: 'I hope, Archpriest, that now the keys are in your hands, you will give them to me without difficulty.'

'You've heard, my dear friend, I'm not the master.'

'And you are listening to Monsieur Turlot, *you*, Monsieur Clamouse?'

'I don't want to make an enemy of Abbé Capdepont. I'm old, and I ask only to be allowed to die in peace.'

'Then the storm must drown the coffin of Monseigneur de Roquebrun?'

'It's not my fault, after all. . . . You understand, my good Lavernède, I am dependent on the capitular Vicar-General and cannot receive this coffin in my house.'

'But just now . . .'

'Ah, you're right, just now . . . but I didn't know that Capdepont . . .'

'That's it: you have greater fear of Rufin Capdepont than of God Himself, for you cannot deceive yourself, Archpriest. Your refusal to give hospitality to your dead bishop is a great offence against God. . . . Oh! I adjure you, don't tremble so wretchedly in this chair. I have no intention of compromising your house. . . . Give me the keys of the cathedral and then resume your whist again, if you please.'

Old Clamouse, tortured by the feeling of cowardice, but incapable of throwing off his terror of Capdepont, made an effort to speak – but he could not.

Lavernède felt moved by a sort of scornful pity. 'Archpriest,' he said, moderating the harshness of his voice, 'I understand your situation, it's extremely difficult. Of course

132

you can't give me the keys of St Irenaeus yourself. But suppose I took them?'

'If you took them from me?'

'I should shift the responsibility. It would fall entirely on me. An eminent casuist like you seems made for appreciating an argument of such importance.'

The old man's eyes came to life. 'Ah, that,' he murmured. 'That's different. It is certain that if by some means you managed to snatch the keys from me . . .'

'Done!' cried Lavernède who, keeping his eyes on the bunch of keys as his prey, took them by a clever, unexpected movement.

'Gentlemen, I protest against this seizure,' murmured old Clamouse, who had felt oppressed by a weight on his chest, and now breathed freely.

'Monsieur Lavernède,' cried Turlot, 'Monsieur Capdepont will be informed at once.'

The look of proud disdain that the triumphant prison chaplain cast at the professor of Holy Scripture silenced the words on his lips.

'Run and denounce me to Rufin Capdepont, sir, run fast! The task of informer is altogether worthy of you.'

He bade goodbye to the young vicars and went out quickly.

XX

THE CATAFALQUE

The fearful storm continued. A strong wind had extinguished the street lamps. The night was thick, dense and horrible. In the sky the same darkness as in the streets. The thunder was silent for a moment; but the noise of water pouring from every side on to the resounding pavement followed like a vast murmur and prolonged the din. In the distance the Arbouse could be heard, from the height of its broken banks, loudly hurtling down its cascades. It went on raining.

However, a light, vague at first then clearer, whitened with its reflection the crowded shadows. At once the seven great windows, light and slender, which make the choir of St Irenaeus a marvel of Gothic architecture, were alight. One by one the elegant rose windows of the side-chapels turned red. Soon the vast mass of the cathedral, all of whose openings were lighted, arose flamboyant, radiant, splendid in the opaque darkness.

After placing the coffin of Monseigneur de Roquebrun on the steps of the high altar, Abbé Lavernède wished to make a mortuary chapel for the dead bishop worthy to avenge him from all affronts. Armed with the keys that opened the drawers in the sacristy which contained every sort of lamp, he had freely helped himself. There was not a candelabrum, not a torch-holder, not a chandelier that did not receive its candle in this strange fête. After an hour of feverish activity it looked as if the interior of St Irenaeus was on fire.

It was in the middle of this blaze, a great contrast with the thick darkness and the confusion of this appalling night, that the religious – Capuchins, Barnabites, Dominicans, Marists – followed by some diocesan priests still faithful to the memory

134

of Monseigneur de Roquebrun, came out of the sacristy and walked in file to the choir of the basilica. Everyone had done his best to hide the disorder of his dress: one had put on a black cloak to cover the mud that had splashed up to his knees, another had exchanged his surplice, soaked to the last thread, with the rochet of one of the prebendaries.

The Provincial of the Capuchins, grave and handsome with his long white beard, walked at the end of the procession. The whole column passed the Bishop's coffin and genuflected, then divided – one part went to occupy the stalls on the right of the high altar, the other to the stalls on the left. The movements were executed in absolute silence, with the majestic gravity that Catholicism can imprint on its ceremonies.

The funeral chants began.

There was truly something grand and terrible about this office for the dead celebrated late at night by a hundred clerics who were afraid of being interrupted in their prayers at any moment by the arrival of Abbé Capdepont. Under the waves of light that fell from the vaults and the walls where many chandeliers were shining, some faces looked uneasy. What would happen if the Vicar-General appeared suddenly in the middle of the nave? Nevertheless, despite the preoccupations that troubled souls and made more than one heart quake, the psalmody went on.

Once an alarming noise shook the building. The columns trembled, the candelabra quivered on the altar steps, and the old walnut stalls groaned. Frightened heads turned towards the door of the cathedral, which had been left open. Was Satan going to invade St Irenaeus? They were reassured; it was the thunder that, before daybreak, hastened no doubt by the sun to finish its work, fired its last canon-bolts into the clouds.

'*Miserere mei . . .*' intoned the Provincial of the Capuchins.

Finally the great window of the choir, imbued with the white light of dawn, allowed its iron casing to be seen. At the same moment on the floor-tiles and on the upper woodwork floated red, blue, green reflections. . . . It was day.

Abbé Lavernède leaned over Abbé Ternisien, crouched in a stall, and said a few words to him in a low voice. The two priests left the places they occupied and went to the sacristy.

'My dear friend,' said the prison chaplain, throwing off a

heavy cloak, 'take off your surplice, and let's go out. There's the sun. Evidently Capdepont won't come to surprise us at present. Who knows? Perhaps the wretched Turlot drew back at the moment of committing an infamy. But we must beware and take precautions. Capdepont may save himself up for the hour of the funeral.'

They left the cathedral and walked towards the Arbouse. They arrived at one of the free-stone bridges. The river was swollen and its reddened, muddy water rushed noisily under the arches. Everywhere the havoc of the night had left its mark: uprooted trees dragged along by the stream, the walls of a factory stranded in the mud, and farther off a mill-race blocked by rocks fallen from the mountains, by heaps of sand and gravel.

However, the day began superbly. The valley of Lormières, washed and garnished by the storm, shone rejuvenated under the sun whose rays pierced the white clouds that still strewed the sky like arrows, and fell down in golden sheaves. The trees of the Corbières were magnificent, showing through a light mist their polished trunks, their shining branches, the luxuriant leaves of a green quite fresh.

The two priests halted at the Quarter of the Paper-Mills.

'I leave you here, my dear Ternisien,' said Lavernède. 'You understand, don't you, how important it is that Monseigneur's poor, and yours, should arrive at the cathedral by nine o'clock? This force will help us to restrain Capdepont and to frustrate his plans if he tries to take the coffin of our bishop to the town cemetery. He won't have the audacity to provoke a struggle, I fear. In any case we shall be in a position to do battle. . . . Go quickly! . . .'

'Then you're not coming with me?'

'I'm running to the rue des Bernardins, to the cathedral architect, to ask him to open one of the tombs in the crypt. Then I shall go to the undertaker's. We want a catafalque such as has never been seen in Lormières and hangings to cover all the walls.'

They separated.

Despite that a hundred workmen were occupied in pulling

cords and driving nails as they put up large black hangings all along the pillars of the nave, it took at least six hours to give the cathedral, now flooded with light, the melancholy atmosphere that the ceremony required. The catafalque alone, raised in the middle of the choir, although the carpentry had been begun the day before, kept the workmen busy for more than two hours. The big, round tiers rose from the pavement, diminishing in size up to the vaults. The whole, crowned by a white-fringed canopy, was covered with black velvet spangled with silver, relieved at the corners by tassels of violet silk, which recalled the costume of the dead man. On the front of this high pyramid, among a forest of flaming candelabra, between two twin crosiers, shone the mitre of Monseigneur de Roquebrun, sparkling with gold and jewels. A little above the glowing mitre a scroll appeared in the midst of the candles with a verse of the Psalms in big letters:

In memoria aeterna erit justus,
Ab auditione mala non timebit.

Abbé Lavernède, that warm, fearless heart, had written these fine words as much as a last homage to the prelate whom he had loved as in defiance of the hatred of Rufin Capdepont.

It struck eleven.

The prison chaplain, who had just been seeing to the final preparations for the ceremony, went to the sacristy, where all the clergy of the town, who had come together at the sound of the bells, waited impatiently. He made a sign to Ternisien. The latter, into whom Lavernède had managed to infuse something of his unconquerable fervour, put himself at the head of the workers massed at the back and led them round the giant catafalque. At least ten rows of chairs had been placed there for the men of the Quarter of the Paper-Mills. This crowd – this army, perhaps – sat down noisily.

'My friends,' said the former private secretary, 'your benefactor is there. We entrust you with the guardianship of him, who loved you to the end.'

'Be at ease. Monsieur Ternisien, we shall not allow the remains of Monseigneur to go out of St Irenaeus to be buried in the town cemetery,' answered the voice of the Vicomte de

137

Castagnerte, who suddenly appeared among the throng of paper-makers, having left General de Roquebrun for a minute with the doctors Barbaste and Leblanc.

The sacristy was crammed with anxious clergy. Why had the capitular Vicar-General not yet arrived? He himself had fixed the hour for Monseigneur's funeral, and that was long past. What was the meaning of this neglect of the simplest propriety?

Those who had been drawn to the cathedral by the hope of being present at some new dramatic scene, showed their complete disappointment in faces tormented by an unhealthy curiosity. Others engrossed by more religious, more noble considerations rejoiced at Capdepont's delay in coming. Perhaps this terrible man, after his hateful tantrums of the previous day, did not dare reappear for fear of being tempted to renew them.

These simple and pious priests, whose confidence in the removal of the danger increased with every minute, were grouped round Abbé Ternisien, and conversed with him in low voices.

The clock in the great tower of St Irenaeus struck one stroke.

'Half-past eleven, my dear **Lavernède**,' said the former private secretary.

'Suppose we begin the mass?' asked the Provincial of the Capuchins.

'No doubt Monsieur Capdepont has given up the idea of presiding at the ceremony,' added the Superior of the Marists.

'I don't think we should wait for him any longer,' broke in the Prior of the Dominicans.

'The coward!' grumbled the prison chaplain, seeing his enemy escape. Then, turning to Monsieur Clamouse, whose anxious eyes were looking all round: 'Would you care to officiate, Archpriest? You are, after Monsieur Capdepont, the first dignitary of the diocese.'

'I can't,' stammered the old man. 'I've already said my mass and . . .'

Abbé Lavernède went to the cupboard, unfolded an amice and, according to custom, offered it to the Provincial of the Capuchins to kiss.

138

'Then it's to you, Reverend Father, that comes the honour of celebrating the holy sacrifice. . . .'

A great noise, caused by a movement of chairs, was heard at the back of the basilica. All eyes turned in that direction.

'Monsieur Mical, gentlemen,' cried Turlot. 'Here's Monsieur Mical!'

In fact the professor of moral theology, his face downcast, and his features contorted by an unknown emotion, entered the sacristy.

'And the Vicar-General?' everyone asked him.

'Gentlemen,' said Abbé Mical, 'Monsieur Capdepont is unwell, very unwell. . . . He is sorry not to come to the cathedral. . . . He would have liked to celebrate the divine office for the memory of Monseigneur de Roquebrun, and himself to give the absolution, but. . . .'

He paused. 'The capitular Vicar-General was already ill yesterday evening,' he went on. 'You must have understood this, gentlemen, from his excited speech, I might almost say from the disorder of his ideas. . . . Who among us does not know the confusion fever induces in our mental faculties? The best minds are not safe . . .'

'Sir,' interrupted Lavernède, boiling with rage, 'if you have come here to decline for Monsieur Capdepont responsibility for the actions he was not afraid to accomplish under our eyes, I must warn you of the uselessness of your words. On this subject the opinion of all the clergy present at that horrible scene is decided, and if Monsieur Rufin Capdepont were to come himself as a suppliant, with a rope round his neck, we should declare ourselves incompetent, not qualified to relieve him from the burden of such a crime.'

'Qualified. . . . What do you mean?'

'I mean it's an unprecedented crime.'

'But your judgement, Monsieur Lavernède . . .'

'Judgement is the word!' cried the prison chaplain. And in a sharp, incisive tone: 'Judgement – it's the Sovereign Pontiff who will pronounce it, when the case comes before his tribunal.'

'Then you've written to Rome?' stammered Mical in amazement.

'Not yet, but one will write.'

Imperiously Lavernède lifted a hand towards the beadle, dressed in his richest mourning uniform. This man, proud as a marshal of France under his embroidery and his silver epaulettes, moved majestically like a column, and let his iron-tipped staff fall on the echoing pavement.

All the priests, religious and secular, walked in step towards the choir forming the procession for the Provincial of the Capuchins, vested in a chasuble with white orphreys.

XXI

THE CLERICAL COMEDY

In the cathedral, humming like a vast hive, the solemn office for the dead was being celebrated with all imaginable ceremony. Meanwhile Messieurs Clamouse, Turlot and Mical, abashed by the importance Lavernède had assumed, chatted in a remote corner of the sacristy.

'Really, one would think he was the master here,' said the Archpriest.

'That's shocking!' exclaimed Turlot.

'Softly, gentlemen!' broke in Mical, with a calm not devoid of melancholy. 'Don't talk so loud. What you fear may very well happen. For my part I shouldn't be surprised if Lavernède were in fact to become our master.'

'He!' said Turlot, with a gesture of contemptuous disbelief.

'Isn't he the great friend of Abbé Ternisien?'

'What does that matter?'

'And if Ternisien were to become Bishop of Lormières?'

Clamouse and Turlot looked at Mical with stupefaction.

'What?' stammered the Archpriest, whose excitement at once died down. . . . 'What are you saying, my friend? It isn't serious, is it?'

'On the contrary, it is very serious, more serious than anything in the world.'

'Good God, you make me tremble, Mical! Explain what you mean, please.'

'What's this old song?' grumbled Turlot.

At the same moment the organ was silent, and a great, full, masterly voice hurled this stanza into the vaults of St Irenaeus:

> *Dies irae, dies illa,*
> *Solvet saeclum in favilla,*
> *Teste David cum Sibylla.*

The three talkers in the sacristy were not in the least moved by these terrifying words, which they were too well accustomed to hear.

'Well?' insisted Clamouse, shaking Mical, who was lost in thought.

'Well, I must tell you that Capdepont has received no news from Paris today. Yesterday night, at about ten o'clock, a telegram came from Monsieur Bonnardot. It said: "The Emperor is to sign the decree tonight. We shall let you know at once if you are nominated." I've been three times to the telegraph office this morning. But nothing, nothing. You can guess what a state Capdepont is in. Just now, when he saw me reappear empty-handed, I thought he was going mad. Ah, it wasn't easy for me to get him to remain in the diocesan office. The struggle was terrible. Look, I bear the marks of it.' The professor of moral theology showed a great bruise that ran across his neck. He went on: 'When I threw myself against the door to prevent him from coming to disturb this ceremony, he suddenly seized me, and I really thought he would strangle me. Lavernède wasn't wrong when he nicknamed Capdepont "Tigrane". Between ourselves, there's something tigerish about that man. Finally, as if afraid of himself, he went back a few steps and sank into an armchair. . . . Gentlemen, I then saw something no one ever saw before. I saw Rufin Capdepont in tears.'

'And you're afraid Abbé Ternisien has been nominated?' asked Clamouse, whose voice was becoming more and more tremulous.

'The emotion that had suddenly touched Capdepont, seemed to me a favourable occasion to make him hear reason. What have I not said! One had at all costs to prevent him from bringing into St Irenaeus the havoc that his hatred, exasperated by the presence of his successful rival, could not fail to make him cause. If he'd shown himself here it would have been a hand-to-hand fight, a battle. There are times when Capdepont becomes a sort of blind force that no one and nothing can master or control. . . . I meant to use this force for the greatness of the Church. My friendship for this man concealed this ambition . . . but I give up. I can do no more.'

The grand voice in the choir chanted:

Mors stupebit et natura,
Cum resurget creatura
Judicanti responsura.

'In short, your conviction is that Abbé Ternisien . . .' went on the Archpriest.

'How often I've prevented Capdepont from ruining himself. But I could do nothing in the court of the bishop's **palace** . . .'

'My dear Mical, let's forget Capdepont and talk about Ternisien. . . . You really believe in his nomination as Bishop of Lormières?'

'How can one doubt it? Doesn't the audacity of Lavernède prove it? Would he have snatched the cathedral keys from your hands yesterday, and just now would he have given orders in the church to your face unless he knew that his friend was becoming bishop and he can trample on us with impunity? . . . Ah, ecclesiastical hierarchy! Is there a chain in the world heavier and more crushing? I already feel the links bruising my flesh. . . . Gentlemen, we have no news from Paris, but be sure that Messieurs Ternisien and Lavernède have received some.'

'Well, I'm in a fine mess, I am,' muttered Clamouse, as if talking to himself.

'And what about me?' interjected Turlot, all his fat shaking in a shiver of fear.

'As far as I'm concerned,' added Mical, 'if Monsieur Ternisien replaces Monseigneur de Roquebrun, all I can do is to ask for my exeat and to leave the diocese. My existence is destroyed, and I owe it to Capdepont.'

'Don't speak of that man!' cried old Clamouse. A flame had put new life into his dull eyes. 'I confess', he went on, 'I feel transported with anger. . . . What a priest, this Capdepont, what a priest!'

'The fault is ours. Why were we so mad as to believe in this insensate ambition?' said Mical. Then, with a gesture of desperate dejection: 'Gentlemen, we have been unfaithful to our character, to our vocation, and we're punished.'

Abbé Turlot let the tears he had been trying to hold back fill his eyes. As for the old Archpriest, he had to lean against the edge of the cupboard; he felt his legs escape from under him.

'My friends,' went on Mical after a long silence, 'let us own

143

that the God who chastens us is still the God of justice. In what has passed in the last month I don't know who – Capdepont, or any of us – has given the most signal proof of moral degradation.'

This admission, which only a priest could have the courage and the simplicity to make, used as he is in confession to probe his own wounds and those of others, earned no reply. Old Clamouse and Turlot were content to bow their heads in shame.

The voice of the choir slowly rolled out this stanza, as heart-rending as a sob:

> *Ingemisco tamquam reus,*
> *Culpa rubet vultus meus;*
> *Supplicanti parce, Deus.*

'Evidently I'll lose my position,' groaned Clamouse.

'Evidently,' answered Mical.

'But how can they proceed against me, for after all I'm a curé of the first class?'

'That's true. You're a curé and in consequence immovable. But your infirmity obliges you to neglect the heavy service of the cathedral, and they'll obtain your retirement from the Ministry.'

'Ah, my poor church that I love so much!'

'Oh, Archpriest, you won't be badly off, you!' muttered Turlot. 'You're a titular canon, and you'll keep your canonry. If only they'll leave me the chaplaincy Monseigneur de Roquebrun granted me in the Hautes Corbières!'

'I don't guarantee anything,' said Mical. 'Lavernède had a bone to pick with you, and that's tiresome for you. Why did you refuse him those wretched keys?'

'But it was you who told me to close the cathedral early,' lamented fat Turlot.

'I! It's quite possible. What would you have done? Capdepont had spoken, one had to obey. For the rest,' he added, raising his fine fox's mask of a head, and looking at his friends with a confidence he had lacked till now: 'I resign myself to the inevitable. Since I have failed in my aim in life, I don't much care what becomes of me. If they let me go and take up my third-class position as curé at Bastide-sur-Mont, if they send me as curate to Harros, the most wretched place in the mountains, if I go into the next diocese – it is more or less the same to me. If Capdepont has sunk me in sinking himself, it is I who wished it.'

'All the same, one must eat, one must live,' mumbled Turlot sadly.

'Live? . . . And what necessity have we to live?' retorted Mical bitterly.

'The deuce!'

'Don't be afraid of anything, Turlot. When you die there'll always be a bit of bread in your bin. One thing really matters: we must become good priests again, as we used to be. Do you remember our ordination, Turlot? What a day! The world was nothing to us, God completely took possession of us.'

The professor of moral theology burst into sobs.

Old Clamouse, who was bored, left Mical and Turlot, who unconsciously had fallen on their knees. He opened a drawer and successively pulled out a fine rochet richly embroidered, then a hood hemmed with a red edge. He put it all on, not without effort. He went to a cupboard, unhooked a stole, and passed it round his neck. He went stealthily to the sacristy door.

'Where are you going so fast, Archpriest?' asked Mical, rising quickly.

'To the choir.'

'To the choir, when the ceremony is over?'

'Better late than never.'

'You can't be thinking of it!'

'On the contrary, I'm certainly thinking of it.'

'But you're too much compromised with Lavernède now.'

'Compromised . . . compromised . . .'

'Monsieur Clamouse, your dignity . . .'

'My dignity? . . . Oh, don't let's confuse a priest's dignity with that of a layman. They have nothing in common.'

Turlot briskly snatched a surplice.

'You too, you're going to the choir?' cried the professor of moral theology, dumbfounded.

'As the Archpriest is going.'

'You're right, Turlot,' said Clamouse.

145

'Look, Archpriest, are you the curé of St Irenaeus?'

'I am, Monsieur Mical.'

'And you consent to go in the train of Abbé Lavernède, who has usurped your functions for the last hour?'

The old man opened his eyes wide in astonishment.

'Listen, Mical,' he said in a tone that he tried to keep firm: 'Turlot and I came to the cathedral to be present at the funeral of Monseigneur de Roquebrun, and we won't allow the influence of Capdepont to prevent us from fulfilling a sacred duty. You, like your terrible friend of the Great Seminary, were only too heavy a burden on the priests of this diocese. Enough of all that nonsense! God at last gives me the force to shake off your hateful yoke, and I shake it off. . . . Thanks to people made to spread hatred, there have arisen, I know, some misunderstandings between the excellent Abbé Lavernède and me. But I'm undeceived now, and see where I was wrong. I'm only waiting for a good opportunity to make my apologies to a priest who has never lost the place I had given him in my heart. As for Abbé Turlot . . .'

'Oh, as for me,' said the fat man, 'I'm not an enemy of Abbé Lavernède. I will add. . . .'

Mical, who was blocking the door of the sacristy, left the way open. He could not listen to any more. Such baseness made him feel sick. In this almost unconscious reaction, which affected all his moral being, he felt that at no moment in all his life of enslavement to Rufin Capdepont had he been so far degraded. How often had he not had the courage to resist the iron will of his tyrant and to break it!

Mical followed with his eyes Messieurs Clamouse and Turlot pushing with difficulty through the crowd of the congregation. When he saw the two square bonnets poised far off in the atmosphere of the church, thickened by burning candles and incense, he returned to the back of the sacristy. His legs no longer supported him; he sat down.

This man, who had given a hand in so many abominable plans, had a moment of supreme disgust. He remained for some minutes sunk in the bitterest, most poignant thoughts. The discouragement into which he had fallen became a light by which to judge others and himself. He looked long into the bottomless pit of clerical misery. Suddenly he rebounded, and these appalling words fell from his lips: 'O Holy Catholic Church! There must be something divine in you, as your priests have not succeeded in destroying you!'

XXII

THE CRYPT

The tower of St Irenaeus, which overtops the round towers of the bishop's palace as a giant overtops pygmies, is a vast, hexagonal monument, bare and severe. As much as the lacework tracery of the cathedral charms one with its flamboyant ornament, so much does the tower depress one with the sight of great walls totally lacking in architectural interest. Ten windows here and there break through the thick masonry, allowing a little light to filter through to the free-stone staircase which every Sunday the chapter's bell-ringer climbs when he goes to pull the bells in order to announce the offices at Lormières. These windows with semicircular arches, and the door cut in a block at the bottom of the heavy building, recall the Roman period and show clearly that the tower of St Irenaeus was built long before the cathedral, in which a gracious, slender, strong Gothic prevails everywhere.

It was towards this Roman door, on whose jambs a rough hand had tried to effect clumsy sculptures of apocalyptic animals, and whose narrow opening led underneath the cathedral, that the priests and the faithful walked in procession, after disengaging the coffin of Monseigneur de Roquebrun from the drapery of the splendid catafalque. Thence they went down into the crypt, an underground chapel where, one after another, sealed by enormous slabs of Pyrenaean granite, are the tombs of the Bishops of Lormières.

The episcopal graves of Lormières did not escape the savage violations of 1793 any more than the royal graves of St Denis. But the first care of Monseigneur de la Guinaudie on taking possession of the see had been to repair the ravages of the Revolution in the crypt, and to have five or six new tombs dug there. In making these funeral monuments, this prelate, who had with difficulty escaped the scaffold, seemed to be telling the people of his diocese: 'More than one bishop expects to die among you. Religion is eternal.'

The procession – regular clergy, canons, simple priests and a very few laymen – entered the narrow staircase. The Abbés Lavernède and Ternisien kept near the coffin, directing the bearers, trying to make them avoid knocks in a twisting passage where the light of the candles barely put the shadows to flight. Finally they reached the crypt.

It was a small church with squat, roughly cut columns and flattened vaults. There were two naves. Only in one place could one distinguish a scriptural text, whose words were peeling off under the permanent damp. Farther on one read *Hic jacet*, still fresh and well preserved, traced by a paintbrush on the tombstone of Monseigneur Grandin, the last bishop buried there.

They placed the coffin at the edge of the open vault. There was a great silence, a cold silence, the silence of death.

Abbé Lavernède, pale but with a resolute air, went up the three steps of the high altar and in a loud voice, which could be heard by the faithful kneeling in the cathedral overhead, he pronounced these words:

In memoria aeterna erit justus,
Ab auditione mala non timebit.

Then, warmly improvising, the former professor of sacred eloquence in the Great Seminary recounted all Monseigneur de Roquebrun's life of charity. He showed him depriving himself of his last resources to succour the poor, walking on foot through the Quarter of the Paper-Mills, simple as an apostle of the early Church, and freely giving alms. 'If there is a needy workman', he cried, 'who hasn't received a visit from our holy bishop and for whom that visit has not been a help, I adjure him to rise and speak aloud.'

But where Lavernède's speech, remaining equally moving, rose to a height adapted to this congregation composed almost entirely of priests was when, judging Monseigneur de Roquebrun in the exercise of his episcopal functions, he came to his everyday relations with the priests of his diocese.

149

'To whom was he not indulgent? Is there one of us who does not cherish the memory of some touching proof of goodness? For my part I have never forgotten that when Monseigneur de Roquebrun thought fit to confide to me a post in Bastide-sur-Mont, I had only to say these words – "What will become of my sick mother?" – for him to give up his plan immediately. Oh, if you had been in the conference chamber! If you had seen his eyes filled with tears! ... Until then, I had admired the dignity of our bishop, his pious and noble character, his inexhaustible charity, his faith which, as Scripture says, would have moved mountains, but henceforth I comprehended that I had not understood that which was best in him – the heart! Man is wretched, he has to be touched to his depths before giving himself entirely to another. So I proclaim in the face of the diocese that the emotion of Monseigneur at the idea of my mother being abandoned was like a flash of light that dazzled me, and that from that day I was attached to him in life as I remain attached to his memory for ever!'

The voice of the prison chaplain had been resonant at first, but little by little it was dimmed by his personal memories. He had to pause for a minute. He went on: 'However, if Monseigneur de Roquebrun had goodness, he had also strength. In granting him the supreme favour of the episcopate, God had at the same time granted him the energy to fulfil its formidable functions. *Omnia possum in eo qui me confortat*, "I can do all in Him who strengthens me," he repeated when, to maintain discipline, he had the painful duty to raise his arm and strike.

'Some have reproached him for severity. But those who saw him preside at the sessions of the diocesan administration, where Death – which comes like a thief – struck him a blow from which he did not recover, know with what benevolence, what sweetness, what humanity he always listened to the accused. No weariness, no disgust in this strong and holy soul could overcome his resolution to arrive at the truth, and to know this shining truth he patiently explored every path, took the depositions of the witnesses, the feeling of the judges, always returning to God by prayer and meditation. And it has been audaciously asserted that this virile nature, just to the

150

point of heroism, precipitated his decisions because of a certain quickness of temper!'

Lavernède's voice, as he grew warmer, had become stronger.

'Brethren,' he continued, 'the character of our late bishop, full of vivacity, strength and firmness, is not unique in the Church. St Paul, St Bernard, St François de Sales were also vigorous apostles. They knew how to arm themselves with severity in order to combat heresy, or to put down revolts that threatened their authority. Who is to blame if Monseigneur de Roquebrun on more than one occasion had to follow the example of these great saints? Have not many seditions broken out in this diocese? On one day, when the wind of anger and vengeance had blown upon us, did we not unite with the deliberate intention of damaging the power and prestige of him whom Jesus Christ, in the fine words of St Thomas, had placed in the midst of us as a shield in Israel, *Christus posuit episcopum super omnes veluti scutum in Israel*?

'O day of sin, day of darkness, day blacker than the morrowless night of Hell, may it be forgotten! May God forgive us the monstrous outrage on which, in an hour of madness, we were bent. May He forgive, above all, him who had the misfortune to conceive the first thought of it. And recognizing that Monseigneur Armand de Roquebrun, thrown by Death from the seat of justice, was just, and that his memory, henceforth protected from calumny, shall live eternally among us, let us repeat this verse of the psalm:

> *In memoria aeterna erit justus,*
> *Ab auditione mala non timebit.'*

The speaker broke off for a minute.

However, having hurled himself on Capdepont as on a prey, having fleshed his cruel tooth in him, and being unable to detach it, Abbé Lavernède was about to go on, but the Provincial of the Capuchins, an old man full of wisdom and prudence, suddenly raised his voice and read the last liturgical prayers in the *Rituale*, and quickly seized the aspergillum.

Surprised in the midst of his frenzied excitement, the prison chaplain was petrified, his mouth remained half open, and his

151

eyes full of confused astonishment. What! They had prevented him from finishing the funeral oration for Monseigneur de Roquebrun. . . . What should he do? Was he to tolerate a silence imposed on him as an affront, just as he had got to the real subject of his discourse? Was the Provincial of the Capuchins in league with Rufin Capdepont?

In the confusion into which he had been thrown by being prevented from uttering all his fiery reproaches of the Vicar-General, he formed cruel doubts – they were hostile to him, they hated him, perhaps they meant to throw him, bound hand and foot, to the vengeance of his enemy? He made a violent spring, and his rough, grey hair bristled on his neck; then, straightening his proud and noble face, he was going to open fire on Capdepont again when a piercing cry, something like the desperate cry of a soul in distress, shook the vaults of the crypt.

'Ternisien!' cried Lavernède, suddenly distracted from his mental aberrations. 'Ternisien!'

At the moment when the Provincial of the Capuchins took a handful of earth and cast it in the pattern of a cross on the coffin of Monseigneur de Roquebrun, now lowered into the vault, the private secretary, giving way to his grief, had opened his mouth and sunk down in a swoon.

'Air, air!' cried the prison chaplain, pushing aside his bewildered colleagues.

The clergy, in great disorder like a scattered flock, rushed for the spiral staircase of the great tower.

Abbé Ternisien, leaning on the arm of Lavernède, and on that of Turlot, who showed a most unexpected alacrity, followed this crowd of frightened priests with short steps.

A minute after this dramatic incident no one was left in the crypt of the cathedral except one man: the sexton of Lormières. He did his work.

On entering the sacristy the former **secretary** of Monseigneur de Roquebrun was installed in an armchair in front of a wide-open window. While the prison chaplain fanned him with the cardboard case of a corporal, the Archpriest Clamouse took off his bands with trembling fingers and with difficulty unbottoned the horse-hair buttons of his collar to ease his breathing.

It was a sight to see how Abbé Turlot, suddenly seized with devotion, fussed about in the sacristy! This fat, apoplectic man had become light as a butterfly, running to all the cupboards, searching for the bottle of white wine kept for the altar, pouring its contents into a glass that he offered to his *dear* Abbé Ternisien, then taking down cloths which he dipped in cold water and humbly handed to Lavernède to dab his friend's forehead.

'What zeal!' sneered Mical, who was watching everything from the dark corner of the sacristy where we left him.

The parish priests of the city, that of St Frument among the first, having heard the voice of the professor of moral theology, surrounded him.

'Monsieur Turlot affirms that Monsieur Ternisien is going to become our bishop. Is that true, Monsieur Mical?' they asked anxiously.

'Don't you see?' he replied, and with a gesture of contempt he showed them the Archpriest and Turlot more or less prostrate at the feet of Ternisien, who had come completely to his senses.

'Thank you, gentlemen, thank you,' murmured the former private secretary in a feeble voice.

'What a fright you gave us!' said old Clamouse, whose dried-up face beamed with a smile. 'For a moment we thought you were dead . . . like the holy bishop we have just buried. . . . Ah, if we had lost you, what a misfortune for us . . . and for all the diocese!'

'The diocese?' interrupted Ternisien.

'Yes, I said "for the diocese",' repeated the Archpriest in honeyed tones. 'Come, I'm not saying anything that isn't serious, and of which I'm not perfectly sure. It was obvious that a man of your merit! . . . Besides, if your profound humility prevents you from understanding me, Messieurs Lavernède and Turlot, I'm certain . . .'

'For my part,' interrupted the prison chaplain, 'I'm sorry, Archpriest, but I don't understand your riddles.'

'And you, Turlot?'

'I think I've guessed your thought.'

153

'Well, my friend?'

'You wish to say, Archpriest, that all the diocese of Lormières wishes Abbé Ternisien to succeed Monseigneur de Roquebrun.'

'There!' said Clamouse with a satisfied air.

'I, to become your bishop!' cried Ternisien. He rose in a fright, and tried to find the sacristy door behind the group, in order to escape.

'You'll be our bishop!' answered old Clamouse with energy.

'You shall be!' added all the parish clergy, suddenly carried away with enthusiasm.

At this instant, when all hearts were beating and all lungs panting, Mical, who had been forgotten, making a real monkey-like leap, jumped out of his hiding-place and rose in the middle of the sacristy, with his arms raised, and cried at the top of his voice: 'The Vicar-General, gentlemen, the Vicar-General!'

XXIII

VIVE MONSEIGNEUR!

In fact Abbé Capdepont was advancing with a slow, majestic step through the cathedral, which was beginning to empty.

He went into the sacristy. He held his head high, but with no air of bravado. His eyes were calm, his face in repose. An impressive serenity, fruit of a soul either profoundly humiliated or completely satisfied, emanated from his whole personality.

In the crowd of clerics the sudden appearance of this dreaded man produced an amazement mixed with terror.

Abbé Mical, burning with curiosity, ran first towards him. 'Has news come from Paris?'

The capitular Vicar-General, entirely given up to thoughts which his impenetrable mask allowed no one to guess, not only made no reply to the professor of moral theology but did not even look at him. 'Is Abbé Ternisien here?' he asked in a voice in which gentle inflections not habitual to him could be discerned.

The former secretary of Monseigneur de Roquebrun, escaping from Lavernède, who was trying to hold him back, made a step towards Rufin Capdepont.

'Monsieur L'Abbé,' said the latter, 'thanks to the earnest care of Dr Mical, I am a little recovered from the sufferings that have tormented me for some days and that this morning were intolerably acute – and I have dragged myself here to renew the apologies that have already been presented to you in my name. I hoped that the funeral ceremony of Monseigneur de Roquebrun was not yet finished, and that perhaps I might be allowed in my capacity as capitular Vicar-General to give the absolution myself. . . . Alas, sir, it would have been painful for me, in paying the last religious tribute over the remains of a prelate like the late Bishop of Lormières, to claim no other right

155

but my hierarchical title. So God, who is both sovereign justice and sovereign mercy, has kept me away from a funeral solemnity at which former misunderstandings with the late bishop made me unworthy to preside.'

These words, pronounced in a respectful tone absolutely strange to Rufin Capdepont, confirmed the clergy of Lormières in the opinion that the terrible Vicar-General was undone. Only a crushing defeat could tear from this proud man the full apology that he was stammering with embarrassment.

An unfriendly rumour arose, and some priests, whom fear had first moved towards Capdepont, did not doubt his disgrace and came back quietly to Lavernède and Ternisien. Mical stayed standing beside the man whom he had tamed and loved. This intriguer had his dignity.

'It is certain, sir, that yesterday evening . . .' murmured old Clamouse, who ventured to look severely at Capdepont.

'In fact,' added fat Turlot, 'it is certain that yesterday evening you passed all bounds.'

'Accuse me, gentlemen, accuse me, all of you!' answered the Vicar-General humbly. 'I am guilty, I am the guiltiest of men. Nevertheless, in spite of errors that sprang from my brain, never from my heart, who appreciated more than I did the high qualities that distinguished our bishop? What authority! What grandeur in his life! Certainly at this hour, more solemn for me than you can realize, I shall not conceal the wrong I did to Monseigneur de Roquebrun. I do not forget the energy with which I opposed certain reforms that he was trying to bring about. I do not forget our contest some years ago when there was a question of making changes in our old liturgy, and when lately he spoke of replacing diocesan priests by religious. But you must admit that it took some courage to strive so valiantly for what I believed to be the truth. . . . I was too persistent, no doubt. But who can boast of always remaining the master of his passions? For my part, in spite of the austerity of a life of work and retirement, I have not always had the power to crush the heads of the thousand cursed serpents that dwell in the bowels of man, born of woman and subject to sin. If ordination, that heavenly favour, mitigates our human failings, it would be sinful pride to believe that it completely suppresses them. . . .

156

Because on more than one occasion you have heard the Demons that each of us has within him hiss by my mouth, that does not mean that I have not struggled against them till I was exhausted, that I have not tried to make heroic efforts to conquer myself entirely for God. Unhappily original sin has set in us infernal resistance to good, and anyone who has plumbed the intimate secrets of human nature knows that this resistance is not the same in everyone. There are men in whom, by a secret plan of Providence, the spirit of Evil has been allowed to make deeper breaches. Born of the Spanish race, so rugged and violent, and yet so Catholic, perhaps I am one of such men. My mother, you should not forget, first saw the light at Varla, a hamlet in the province of Biscay – and I am like my mother, a nature of iron for the earth, and fire for Heaven. . . . Gentlemen, one must be indulgent to unfortunate people doomed to live perpetually under arms, and to win the last quiet of death by a life without truce or rest.'

'Instincts perverted by sin, and the place where we were born, cannot excuse our misconduct,' said Lavernède.

'Sir,' replied Capdepont with sovereign calm, 'I think the time for clemency has come. When I wish to be pacific, what will you gain, pray, by reviving passions that will be mine no more? St Augustine said: "I have thrown far away from me the old man, like rags and tatters, and I shall not put him on again!" I have made the same vow as St Augustine. The deeds of which you remind me, Monsieur Lavernède, and which I condemn as you do, were done, I call God to witness, in sickness, in fever, in delirium. I hardly remember them. I do recollect, however, that I summoned you to appear before the diocesan tribunal. Don't come, my brother, and forgive me as I forgive you.'

Then he continued, turning up his eyes: '*Cor contritum et humilatum, Deus non despicies* – My God, you will not despise a humbled and contrite heart.'

The prison chaplain was quite dumbfounded, faced with such repentance and such high reasoning. He distrusted Rufin Capdepont, and yet felt himself half conquered. . . . What a change! . . . Perhaps the Vicar-General, simultaneously annihilated and enlightened by the crushing blow of his repulse, would finally, at the age of fifty, return to a sane priest's life, and to charity. What eloquent grief when he had spoken of his terrible conflicts with the Demons! And his mother, that rustic St Theresa. . . .

Lavernède, that loyal heart, spontaneous and sincere, after all the violence they had exchanged, wished to throw himself into his enemy's arms. He was fascinated. He made a step. Then, looking fixedly, he stopped suddenly. Doubt seized him again in front of Capdepont's superhuman placidity.

'One thing in our late bishop', went on the capitular Vicar-General, 'which I always praised without reserve, was his attitude towards the Holy See. Never did the diocese of Lormières have a more Roman pontiff. Knowing what bitterness falls daily to the lot of the Successor of the Apostle he neglected no opportunity of giving him the clearest marks of his submission, his respect and his unalterable attachment. For Monseigneur de Roquebrun the ship of Peter, attacked by storms, was the whole Church, and we have seen him weep when amid the outrage of contemporary politics he feared to see the disappearance of the holy ark which bears the soul and salvation of humanity. This ardent love of Monseigneur de Roquebrun, which was not the sole greatness of his episcopate, will remain an example to the successor whom it will please God to give him.'

'His successor . . . his successor . . .' interrupted the Archpriest, grown more courageous. 'We know his successor.'

'May God grant him the grace necessary for the accomplishment of his difficult mission . . .'

'God is with him, Monsieur Capdepont, don't worry.'

The Vicar-General, after his ultramontane declaration – too unexpected not to have a connection with some hidden plan – turned slowly and made a few steps towards the great oak press. As his words and gestures no longer interested anyone, the clergy, in haste because it was lunch-time, went towards the door of the sacristy.

Monsieur Clamouse had passed his arm through that of Abbé Ternisien. 'Come, friend,' said he. 'Courage! . . . Come and have something at my house. Who knows, perhaps you have need of food?'

'One moment, gentlemen. I have two words to add,' said Rufin Capdepont.

'We'll listen to you another time!' cried the shrill voice of Turlot.

'Another time . . . another time . . .' repeated Clamouse.

'Stop!' cried the Vicar-General, in that arrogant, harsh voice of command that everyone knew well.

Everyone stayed still, and eyes full of uneasy surprise turned towards Capdepont.

He, meanwhile, preserved a stately attitude. He stood up straight again, for he had bowed to Ternisien, and he had regained his old proud demeanour. All the same it might be guessed from his more careless pose that an unknown hand – was it the Demon or the finger of God? – had touched this inflexible bar, and that it could now bend, or undulate like a reed. The folds of his soutane fell straight to his feet, draping him with the marble rigidity of a statue, but evidently this statue had bowels and a heart.

Capdepont's chest, which one could have thought slender, seemed suddenly enlarged, to absorb more air and breathe more freely. Above all, his head seemed transfigured. Certainly there were still those fine sculptural lines full of nobility which held our attention at the beginning of this study; but on this priest's face, always in motion, instead of reading anxiety, bitterness and the brutal disdain of a superior, one found indulgence, sympathy, almost goodness. His eyes, hearths whence so many criminal flames sprang, still shone like beacons in the shade of his thick brows, but their brightness was singularly moderated; no more sinister flashes, but a dimmed light, something tender, benevolent and affectionate. Even his abundant hair, whose locks the previous day had shaken like serpents with the rough obstinacy of an atrocious vengeance, now surrounded his face with grey, vaporous, almost transparent waves, and gave it the character of heavenly resignation and ideal sweetness. Round that forehead, seat of a magnificent intelligence, the cloud of this silver hair was like a saint's halo or a king's crown.

'Gentlemen,' said Capdepont, with an emotion that he could not contain and that made his audience shiver, 'it was not only to offer my excuses to Abbé Ternisien and to deplore in public the disputes that arose between Monseigneur de Roquebrun

159

and the Superior of the Great Seminary that I have come to St
Irenaeus. . . .' He paused.

'And what more?' asked Mical quickly.

Abbé Capdepont lowered his long, tawny eyelids over eyes
fervent as an eagle's, and was silent.

'We beg you to speak, Vicar-General,' repeated the
professor of moral theology, who felt pins and needles all over
his body.

'Speak, speak!' cried all mouths, turned like eyes towards
Capdepont.

Then the capitular Vicar-General uttered these words with a
slowness that allowed him to stress every syllable: 'Gentlemen,
the second motive which has brought me to the cathedral is,
like the first, penitential. . . . Am I worthy, indeed, of the
august ministry to which God has just called me? . . . *Domine
non sum dignus*. . . . My brothers, my friends, my children –
for there are young ones among you whom I shall love like a
father – in receiving the news this morning that I have been
nominated bishop of this diocese . . .'

'You are!' cried Mical, who could not hold back that cry.

'I have thought of one thing only, to come and weep for my
faults, to come and humble myself at the feet of the altars.'

'Vive Monseigneur!' cried Mical, transported with joy.

'Vive Monseigneur!' repeated the diocesan priests.

The Archpriest Clamouse, having abruptly left the arm of
Abbé Ternisien, had at length come without encumbrance in
front of Capdepont. 'Vive Monseigneur!' he stammered, with
what remained of his strength, 'Suppose we sang a *Te Deum*?'
he added.

'Not yet, gentlemen, not yet,' Lavernède interposed
vehemently. His voice echoed like a bugle in the sacristy.

The Bishop Elect of Lormières let fall a sharp look on his
enemy. Guessing that the struggle was near he thought only of
fortifying himself in the unmoved calm he had so skilfully
adopted, and from which he promised himself he would not
depart.

Perhaps, in spite of the great provision of strength that he
had stored up, Capdepont was sorry to have left the bishop's
palace to dare this last adventure. The truth is that on receiving
from Paris the telegram signed 'Bonnardot' he had felt almost

dazzled, and rushed to St Irenaeus without thinking, almost without knowing what he did, pushed by that selfish feeling of human nature which makes us cry out our good luck to others, in order to humiliate them and make them suffer. Is not our triumph the abasement of those around us? And is it not delightful to be put by fortune in a position to show oneself cruel, and to be envied!

It was only as he broke through the crowd which obstructed the cathedral that Rufin Capdepont felt sobered and came to his senses again. The idea of retreating came to him. It was not possible, for he had certainly been seen. 'I shall go there,' he said, his eyes fixed on the door of the sacristy, 'but I shall behave like a bishop.'

And now, with the prison chaplain entering the lists to exasperate him and carp at him, his humour, so apt to fits of passion, was calmed by this thought that flattered it deliciously: I'm no longer the Abbé Capdepont, I'm Monseigneur Rufin.

'Gentlemen,' he said. 'Abbé Lavernède is right. The civil power, which is not much, has nominated me. But the Holy Father, who is everything, hasn't yet elected me. So I will beg you to join your prayers with mine that God may enlighten the Sovereign Pontiff in the choice that must be made of your bishop.'

'The Sovereign Pontiff, be sure, will be enlightened about the smallest details of your life,' interjected the prison chaplain.

'Are you thinking of being my accuser, Monsieur Lavernède?'

'I warn you, a voice against you will arise in Israel.'

'You are implacable.'

'Were you not implacable for ten years towards Monseigneur de Roquebrun – "Bishop Roquebrun", as you contemptuously called him?'

'Sir!' cried Capdepont, shaken in his impassivity by this blow.

'I told you yesterday I'm not afraid of you,' said the prison chaplain, pushing aside the priests who were trying to hold him back, and walking straight towards the Vicar-General.

The latter, whose whole temper was rising, lowered his eyes so as not to see his enemy. Perhaps he was afraid of not being able to resist the fearful temptation to throw himself forward and strike him. Had not Mical accused Capdepont of sometimes hurling himself forward like a blind force? What a struggle it would be if the mountaineer of Harros, pacified for the moment by the feeling of satisfied ambition, could no longer bridle his passions and they rushed out like wild beasts with gaping jaws and claws outstretched!

It was evident that at that moment Rufin Capdepont made the most determined battle of his life against his instincts in revolt. His knees, so firm, now made little convulsive movements under his soutane. His hands were stuck in a nervous grip into a single clasp, something as alarming as a club. The fire of anger disfigured the statue whose harmonious proportions we have admired, and seemed to dislocate it. The head of our hero, that proud head, fell on his chest so that the convulsion which no doubt appeared on his face completely escaped all eyes.

What was passing inside it?

Finally, the Vicar-General raised his handsome forehead and, to everyone's amazement, he showed a calm, almost smiling face. La Bruyère has written: 'Nothing so much refreshes the blood as having been able to avoid a folly.' In fact there was an air of refreshment in Rufin Capdepont's peaceful features. He had triumphed over himself.

'Monsieur Lavernède, what have I done to you that you should persecute me like this?' he said, in a voice choked with tears.

'To me, nothing. But you are a threat to the Church.'

'The Church, for which I am ready to die!'

'And to live,' added the prison chaplain with sarcasm.

Capdepont turned pale, and as if overcome by faintness he leaned suddenly on the arm of Mical, and pressed it with a clenched hand. He was at the end of his tether. He had used up all his strength, and now appealed for help, feeling unable to sustain any longer the role of resigned victim. Blood like a sea was raging in his chest. He would be carried away by the flood. Mical, the clever, shrewd, instinctive Mical, understood the vigorous, burning touch of his friend. He had to save him.

'Gentlemen,' he said, 'Monseigneur Capdepont is ill . . . I recognize the signs that precede the attacks to which he has

162

been subject for several days. . . . Monseigneur needs rest. . . .
Monseigneur will receive you all presently. Monsieur L'Abbé
Turlot, kindly run to ask my brother the doctor to go at once to
the office of the bishop's palace. I'm afraid Monseigneur may
have need of his help. Go quickly.'

'My friends, pray for me, pray for me,' repeated the new
Bishop of Lormières going through the rows of priests, who
looked at him with touched interest.

'What a comedian!' Lavernède could not refrain from
murmuring.

Capdepont heard him, but his bowed body did not even give
a shiver. 'My Reverend Fathers,' he said in a low voice,
addressing himself to the Superiors of the religious orders, 'if
you write to Rome, beg your generals to declare to the Holy
Father that my health is very bad, and that I fear to be unable to
support the crushing duties of the episcopate. Alas! My life is
attacked at its source, but I shall die with my eyes turned
towards the chair of Peter, which has always had the affection
of my heart and the submission of my spirit.'

Meanwhile the majority of the priests of the city, whom the
Archpriest Clamouse had no need to urge, accompanied the
poor, sick bishop through the cathedral, and he retired,
harassed by the prison chaplain.

When he came opposite to the catafalque of Monseigneur de
Roquebrun, where some stumps of candles threw a flickering
light as they burned away in their silver sconces, Rufin
Capdepont stopped. He bowed, and then gravely made the
sign of the cross. For Lavernède this mummery, in front of the
mitre and crosier he had so greatly coveted, seemed like a
profanation. He could not restrain himself, and this cry of
execration escaped him: 'Cain, what have you done with your
brother?'

But Rufin Capdepont, whom Mical held more tightly, made
no answer to this ferocious accusation. He bowed a little lower
on the arm of his faithful acolyte, and went unsteadily out of St
Irenaeus. As no information had yet come from Rome, and his
appointment remained in doubt, the hour had not yet come for
this new Sixtus V to cast aside his crutches, to stand up at his
full height and impose respect or terror on his enemies.

XXIV

THE EVASION

There was a great stir in the little town under the Corbières.
The pious women who long since had been captivated by the
grand, despotic air of the Vicar-General went from door to
door singing in a low voice as on the eve of Easter 'Alleluia!
The Abbé Capdepont is Bishop of Lormières. Alleluia,
alleluia!'

But he was nowhere to be seen. The sort of officious people
who are attracted by any eminence – priests and laymen –
crowded the court of the bishop's palace to offer their
congratulations to his lordship. Mical, on sentry duty at the
office door, invariably told them: 'Monseigneur is unwell. He
can't receive anyone – doctor's orders.'

This incorruptible gaoler, who saw his own grand vicariate
as depending on the episcopate of his friend, was protecting the
benefit of another in order to protect his own, and hardly
allowed Capdepont to take part in the entertainment which, on
his return from Paris, the Baron Thévenot gave in his mansion
on the banks of the Arbouse in honour of his son's former
tutor. The new bishop, moreover, showed remarkable
circumspection on the occasion. The Baron and his wife,
delighted at having 'made a bishop', made vain attempts to
rouse him in one way or another, hoping to induce him to
make a speech, which would have been an honour to this house
where once he had come so poor and humble; but he did not
deviate from his reserve. Instead of mingling with the laymen
invited, among whom Madame Thévenot's vanity hoped to see
him distinguish himself, Capdepont, who had examined the
group of white ties with a furtive glance, perceived the
arrogant, mocking face of the Vicomte de Castagnerte, and fell
back upon the clergy who had accompanied him, the
Archpriest Clamouse, the Abbés Turlot and Mical and others,

and persisted in remaining with them. Even in this friendly circle he made few remarks: two words about his wretched health, a phrase about the Holy Father, who had all his respect and submission – that was all.

In adopting this line of conduct where prudence had the better of guile, Capdepont was obeying the first law of his interest. In fact he had never been surrounded by more snares; his enemies had never worked against him with more implacable anger. Not only had Lavernède, faithful to a hatred whose source was in religious feeling, roused the Paper-Mills against Monsieur Bonnardot's protégé, but every day more and more he alienated the Quarter of the Convents against him. There the Vicomte de Castagnerte reigned as absolute master, and gave impetus to the damage.

Soon the hostility of the city became so evident that Capdepont, resolved to avoid the workers of the Paper-Mills, who were capable of every sort of attack, no longer dared to go out of the Great Seminary to the offices of the bishop's palace where the diocesan business called him every morning.

Certainly it was not without annoyance that the mountaineer of Harros, violent to a frenzied degree, resigned himself to a sequestered life; and more than once the cloister of the Minims, where he walked alone with Mical in stormy melancholy, resounded with cries torn from him by the affronts made to his character, his dignity, his high station. But what could be done in the face of the public opinion excited against him? In order not to see fall from his head the mitre that had just been put there, this untameable man had to learn to conquer himself, until he was allowed to bring his rough hand down heavily on others in order to bend them and oblige them to ask for mercy.

However, if Abbé Lavernède had made the terrible Capdepont lie on a bed of thorns, he himself did not sleep on a bed of roses. At Lormières all went very well; but in Rome? . . . There was no news from there. It was nearly a month since the reports from the Provincial of the Capuchins, of the Prior of the Dominicans, of the Superior of the Marists had gone, and there was no reply. Were they going to take no notice of so many important documents, signed by persons of such authority?

165

To crown all, Abbé Ternisien, a man of a delicate nature and little energy, delayed indefinitely his departure for Rome, though he decided to return to his convent at Tivoli. This young priest, who hated every sort of strife and dispute, trembled at the mission with which they would not fail to charge him, and waited in hope of avoiding the task. Certainly he believed Capdepont unworthy of the episcopate; for the honour of the Church he would have wished that a strong hand might seize this rebel by the neck and chase him roughly from the dignity he was going to usurp. But as to becoming himself that firm grip, capable of pulling out of the temple the proud, cunning, vindictive Vicar-General, he had neither the strength nor the will. He put off leaving Lormières, he went on putting it off. . . .

'We must go!' So one morning said the prison chaplain, who suddenly appeared in front of him, with bloodshot eyes and a face of fury.

'My God, what's happened?'

'I've come from Father Trézel. Despite my almost unconquerable reluctance, and my small hopes of convincing this Jesuit, I went to beg him also to make a step towards his general. "It's evident", I said to myself to get up my courage on entering the College of St Stanislas Kotska, "that Capdepont will collapse if I succeed in throwing against him the most powerful corporation in the Christian world . . ." '

'And you failed?'

'Not only have I failed, not only have I got nothing from this crafty father, but having succeeded – not without some cunning, I confess with shame – to pump him, I thought I was to understand, from a certain reticence on his part, that it isn't against Rufin Capdepont that they're instituting proceedings in Rome . . .'

'What, then?'

'Against me, and you above all, my dear friend.'

'Me!' cried Ternisien, growing horribly pale.

' "In the apostolic offices they are surprised to find, mixed up in the wretched quarrels of Lormières, the name of a young priest who had left a good impression in Rome, and to whom the Holy Father himself had deigned to accord signs of his

166

good will" – that's how Father Trézel expressed himself, without ever looking one in the face.'

Poor Abbé Ternisien could not get over his surprise.

'It's too much!' he said, with a gesture of anger.

'These are the sort of tricks Capdepont, Mical and the Superior of St Stanislas Kotska know how to play, for henceforth we must think of them together. . . . That's it, the Vicar-General has been turned into a victim, and Messieurs Lavernède and Ternisien become the calumniators of this poor unfortunate who cannot defend himself. . . . What a shame, indeed! Ah! poor Catholic Church. However, if one didn't believe in a just God! . . .'

The prison chaplain cast up to Heaven a look in which all the anguish of his soul was blazing.

'God has no part in the intrigues plotted by the Demon,' stammered Ternisien, with the robust faith of simple people and the saints.

There was a silence.

'Do not let us allow ourselves to be crushed, my friend,' went on Lavernède in a resolute tone. 'We must strive to the end, for God and His Church. . . . Go. There you'll see Cardinal Maffeï . . . who, by a piece of good luck beyond hope, seems to have been chosen by the Roman Curia to study the Capdepont affair. The Cardinal knows you. He will listen to you and you will enlighten him. . . . You know what unbreakable ties keep me in Lormières. Well, if I had the contacts in Italy that you can turn to decisive account in our cause, I would leave my mother and fly to the help of the Church, that other mother, whom we love like devoted and jealous sons.'

'I'll go tomorrow.'

'Let us make haste. Monsieur de Castagnerte, when I met him in the rue St Frumence, thinks Capdepont left Lormières some time ago. Mical is always standing at the door of the Great Seminary, and his brother the doctor never neglects his daily visit to the Minims' cloister. But it's a farce, intended to disguise the absence of Capdepont. . . . A peasant of the neighbourhood – some weeks ago – walking at night on an out-of-the way path on the mountain, met a tall priest who

167

walked with great strides, talking to himself and making exaggerated gestures. Evidently it was Capdepont. Anxious to conceal his departure, he was going by foot to some place in the hills. Where was he going? No doubt to Paris to pester the Nuncio, and to rouse all his friends . . .'

'I'll go tonight,' said Ternisien with energy.

XXV

CARDINAL MAFFEI

Monseigneur de Roquebrun's former secretary arrived in Rome towards the middle of August, in fact on the eve of the Assumption. He went to the Theatine Fathers in the monastery of St Andrea della Valle, where he had many friends, and stayed there several days. Finally, a little recovered from the fatigue of the journey, and having summoned up sufficient courage, he went one afternoon towards the Vatican and knocked on the door of the Palazzo Candia, where Cardinal Maffeï lived.

Abbé Ternisien did not have to wait long. It was his eminence himself who, breaking with the etiquette much in favour in the houses of prelates where everything is done as ceremoniously as in church, came to find him in his seat in the ante-room.

'My dear child, my dear child!' said Monseigneur Maffeï, embracing him effusively.

Our young priest, whose heart beat loudly, followed the Cardinal into the large room which served as his study.

His eminence the Cardinal was an old man of about seventy-five. He held himself a little bent, but one guessed that his height must be above the average. His head, almost completely bare, shone like polished ivory. A few rare white hairs above his ears and at the bottom of the nape of his neck recalled his former monastic crown, for he had been the Superior of the Franciscans of Tivoli. His face, with acute angles dominated by a big long nose like that of St Charles Borromeo, was pale, and had an imposing character of ascetic coldness. He walked slowly, as becomes those who wear purple.

The Cardinal showed a chair to Ternisien, and sat down. 'At last you have come back to us,' he said kindly.

169

'And for good, your eminence.'

'So much the better. You have been much missed at Tivoli. When I announced your return to the General of the Franciscans, who came to see me this morning, he seemed quite delighted.'

'Your eminence had then been told of my coming arrival?' asked Ternisien, too honest to conceal his surprise.

'Don't I know all that happens in the Christian world?' answered the Cardinal with a smile.

'But I had not written to anyone.'

'And my little finger?' said Monseigneur Maffeï, lifting his beautiful, pale, slender, clerical hand. 'No, I heard only yesterday from the Jesuits at the Gesù that you had come or were coming to Rome.'

'At the Gesù. . . . Ah! I remember Père Trézel . . .'

'That is in fact the name of the Father whose long report on that little clerical scuffle at Lormières was read to me. . . . But, my child, there was a lot about you in that rigmarole. . . . You were up to tricks, it seems, with your friend . . . your friend. . . . Help me please . . .'

'The Abbé Lavernède.'

'Yes, the Abbé Lavernède. . . . What a hot-headed man is that Lavernède!'

'You are not mistaken, Monseigneur. The Abbé Lavernède, who is my friend, has a vigorous hatred of sin, and is unable to keep cool when faced with it. I, who lack his courage, have often reproached him for his too implacable attack on Evil. "You will get yourself into an unfortunate scrape," I have told him a hundred times – to tell the truth, I never thought I was so good a prophet.'

The Cardinal watched Ternisien speak these words with passion. When he had finished, he continued to observe him attentively.

'Take care, my dear abbé,' he said. 'I have precise information about all that happened at Lormières. To excuse your friend's errors, you must not . . .'

'If your eminence will kindly allow me to give him a faithful account.'

Poor Ternisien's voice faltered, and big tears ran down his face.

The Cardinal, an old diplomat, whose heart had long been

dried up in the discussion of affairs, remained cold in front of this youthful emotion. He made a polite gesture to invite Monseigneur de Roquebrun's former secretary to explain himself, and never said a word.

Then Abbé Ternisien related the whole episcopate of Monseigneur de Roquebrun and the implacable opposition of Rufin Capdepont. He did not leave out one circumstance in the long martyrdom of his friend and protector. More than once he quoted verbally the rudeness of him whom he ventured to call the 'butcher' of the last Bishop of Lormières.

The Cardinal listened impassively, leaning towards the speaker so as not to lose a word.

In vain Ternisien paused several times, trying to see on the face of his eminence some effect of the emotion that moved him so violently; the impenetrable, even icy mask of the attentive old man did not reveal anything of his impressions.

Although embarrassed by a silence that indicated unfavourable prejudice, our young priest went on bravely, seeing his own honour and that of his friend Lavernède at stake. Soon he got to the horrible scene of Monseigneur de Roquebrun's coffin in the court of the bishop's palace, surrounded by the clergy and chapter of Lormières.

This time the Cardinal seemed to be affected, for he lifted his head slightly and looked fixedly at Ternisien. 'This thing happened exactly as you're telling me?' he asked severely.

'I call God to witness.'

'Good. I believe you. Go on.'

'I have no more to add, Monseigneur.'

'I beg your pardon. You haven't reported the last scene in this little melodrama – not edifying, I agree, but less terrible than it is imagined in Lormières. The scene of which I want to remind you is that in which your Abbé Lavernède, in the very cathedral of St Irenaeus, ventured to throw in the Vicar-General's face the accusation – difficult to justify – of having killed Monseigneur de Roquebrun.'

'Abbé Lavernède, in front of the catafalque of the late bishop, only cried: "Cain, what have you done with your brother?" '

'That seems to me enough, and I say no more.'

'The heat of the strife might perhaps excuse . . .'

171

'No. . . . Observe, at the moment when this Abbé Lavernède insulted the capitular Vicar-General to this degree, the latter had just been nominated bishop, which ought to make him sacred to everyone. Respect for the hierarchy is part of the strength of the Church.'

'Will your eminence allow me to confess that for Monsieur Lavernède . . . and for others, it is the canonical institution that makes bishops, not the designation by the civil power, which has no religious character? My friend did not believe that the telegram received that same morning from Paris protected Abbé Capdepont from the terrible responsibility he had incurred.'

'Your friend was wrong. We, who sign concordats with all the sovereigns of the earth, know what we ought to think of the authority of the laity, but we are far from showing the proud contempt for it of a little cleric of Lormières. Certainly the bishops who come from the North and the South are not all equally agreeable to the Holy Father. But his holiness has a very clear idea of the situation in which the Church is placed, and it is rare that he does not ratify the choice of governments. Monsieur Lavernède is intelligent. He is not ignorant of the peculiar discretion to which the Holy See is obliged in regard to France, and he has been guilty of provoking a scandal which, but for the prudence of Monsieur L'Abbé Capdepont, could have been the subject of a most regrettable conflict between Paris and Rome.'

This was a reprimand for Ternisien in the rather hard tone in which the last words were pronounced. The young priest understood, and at once felt frozen.

Again, the former private secretary of Monseigneur de Roquebrun was not made for strife. When he saw weighing on him and on his friend, with whom he generously identified himself, such odious imputations, he feeling of justice was revolted, and he could have said some sharp words. But as all effort was useless and iniquity was triumphant, only one course was left him to follow, that of resignation. Thus natures that are too feeble or too much absorbed in charity give up the noblest causes, and leave an easy victory to the wicked. Too absolute adoration, whether of God or of oneself, often produces identical results.

172

Ternisien, terrified by the Cardinal's attitude, was henceforth on the watch for the first pretext which would allow him to make an honourable retreat. Oh, with what joy would he leave this perverse world and flee to solitude in Tivoli! At this moment of utter discouragement the young Franciscan savoured in thought the happiness of the religious life, in a secluded cell, far in the desert! Oh, the annihilation!

Monseigneur **Maffeï**, whose inquisitorial eye followed all the incertitudes, fears and eagerness of the weak man sitting in front of him, was moved to pity. With an affectionate movement he took his hands in his own and pressed them. At this contact Ternisien, drowned in an ocean of bitterness, revived with a start and, embarrassed by the long silence, stammered this question: 'Then, Monseigneur, do you think that his holiness will sanction the appointment of Abbé Capdepont?'

The Cardinal got up sharply. 'What!' he cried with an anger not unmixed with irony. 'Because at Lormières, a village at the end of the world, some diocesan priests and some religious gave themselves the not very charitable satisfaction of provoking the impetuous, perhaps too impetuous nature of Abbé Capdepont beyond endurance, the Church is to be deprived of the great advantages that this nature, led, moderated and modified by her, is capable of affording her? Really, sir, I am astonished at the pretensions of the people who have sent you. . . . Yes, it is extraordinary presumption! . . . And since when, pray, has it been the affair of simple clerks to mix themselves up in questions that concern only the Holy Father, or those to whom he has delegated them without appeal? It's a complete reversal of the hierarchy. . . . If you, Frenchmen, love revolution, we Romans detest it with all our hearts and, refusing to risk adventures, we remain immobile on the rock, *super petram*, where the hand of God has placed us. . . . Take your choice, Monsieur L'Abbé. The candidate presented by your government for the see of Lormières will be canonically instituted. It is not that we have more regard than is proper for your emperor, whose object, we know well, is to abase the French episcopate, hoping to dominate it more easily when he has filled it with incapable members. But information from the Nunciate in Paris, and elsewhere, shows us Abbé

Capdepont as a priest of great merit and the highest virtue. Among others, he has one superior quality which the Church should take into account in these times when the civil powers are capable of audacity, villainy and perversity – he is courageous. Abbé Capdepont – there is a character! Would to Heaven that the pastoral crook might always fall into hands so strong and so devoted!'

'May I venture to observe to your eminence that this devotion to the Holy See is of somewhat recent origin? For formerly. . . .'

'That is an error. The Vicar-General of Lormières submitted to civil authority, he never loved it. He was to become a bishop. God, who reserved to him a mission in His Church, had for long past put in his flesh and bone, to use a vigorous biblical expression, the feeling of His strength, and if to fulfil an ambition from which Heaven was to benefit he had to throw some crumbs of flattery to your Ministry of Ecclesiastical Affairs, fundamentally he knew the wretchedness of what in politics they call "established power" and he despised it. He seemed to be submissive in Paris, but in reality it was to Rome that he was submissive. It was for the sake of Rome that he humbled himself, so far as to pretend, sometimes even to . . . lie.'

'To lie? Monseigneur? To lie,' repeated Ternisien, scandalized.

'Well! What's up with you? And what absurdly narrow meaning do you attach to that word? Ah, one sees very well that you have been away from us for ten years! Don't you understand our language any more? The Church never lies, never! It isn't within the capacity of the Church, Truth itself, to lie. But the Church, which has been at strife, in primitive times with the last pagan princes, in the Middle Ages with half-barbarian kings, in our own days with the whole world, has constantly had the need of suppleness and shrewdness to pursue her divine mission through the centuries. The Cardinals Caprara and Consalvi, harassed by General Bonaparte, who was capable of provoking a schism in France, were forced to lie to him more than once, as Abbé Capdepont, entangled in the Gallican intrigues of Napolean III, lied to him. . . . But, I ask you, sir, is one lying when, in spite of men determined to exile

God from the world, one uses the resources, the delicacy, even the subtlety of one's mind to maintain the rule here below of Him who is the way, the truth and the life – *Ego sum via, veritas et vita.*'

Ternisien was overcome with perplexity. He looked at Cardinal Maffeï, who had just sat down again, with a frightened expression.

'And then how gifted Abbé Capdepont is!' went on the old prelate, carried away by enthusiasm. 'I wish you had been at St Louis des Français on the feast of the Assumption, and that you had heard him.'

'What? Monsieur Capdepont is in Rome?'

'He had the great honour to preach the panegyric of the Blessed Virgin before the Holy Father and all the Sacred College. What elevation! What warmth in his speech! – "I fancy I am listening to St Bernard," the Cardinal Vicar murmured several times. . . . On the afternoon of that great day his holiness deigned to receive Abbé Capdepont in order to give him his congratulations in person. . . . My dear Ternisien, if you had seen this man whom you like so little in the salons of the Vatican, his easy manners, his stance at the same time modest and proud, you would agree with me that God had granted him such astonishing dignity only because he had from long past reserved for him a high destiny. "The mitre will look becoming on that head," said the Holy Father to the General of the Jesuits, who accompanied the newcomer. Then, embracing Abbé Capdepont, who knelt at his feet, Pius IX deigned to call him "My brother".'

'Then all is over?'

'All is over, my child. The Abbé Capdepont – I authorize you to send the news to Lormières – will be appointed in the consistory to be held on the eighth of next month, the feast of the Nativity of the Blessed Virgin.'

Ternisien rose, profoundly saluted his eminence, and without a word went towards the door of the study.

'You go away like that, without murmuring a farewell?' said the Cardinal.

The young priest returned, made two steps towards Monseigneur Maffeï, and suddenly fell on his knees before him.

The old prelate rose, gravely stretched out a hand and made the sign of benediction. 'Look, child,' he said kindly, raising Ternisien. 'Be forgiven for your peccadillo, and don't do it again. Leave the business of the Church to those on whom God has laid the burden. Presently, in our adorable Tivoli, where your brothers are expecting you, you'll find peace and quiet. Why is it not granted to me to follow you? . . . Are you not happier than I? . . . Why hasn't the Holy Father left me there among you? Ah, I would gladly exchange my purple for my serge habit of old days! . . . If you knew what business is, and how little men love justice! What is the dignity of a cardinal worth compared with the peace I enjoyed? In Tivoli I was novice, then friar, then superior – what happiness!'

Monseigneur **Maffeï**, moved by the remembrance of his youthful years of simple and modest piety, broke off.

He soon went on again, in an energetic voice.

'But remember, my very dear Ternisien, that if regulars and secular priests are needed for the triumph and heavenly splendour of the Church, courageous bishops are also needed to defend her. This naturally brings me back to Abbé Capdepont, and I find myself obliged to tell you that in this deplorable affair of Lormières you, your friend Lavernède, and the superiors of religious orders who sent reports to Rome, have confused two things which at no period of ecclesiastical history ever had anything in common – the Church and the government of the Church. The Church is still today what she always was: divine, infallible, above human chances and changes. As for her government, required from the first to fight against every form of culpable enterprise, particularly against the covetousness, corruption and harshness of princes, so marked in our time, she has more than once been obliged to place at her head chiefs more firm than pious, more energetic than prudent, and to all appearance more animated by the spirit of the world than by that of Heaven. But would the Church have survived had not God sent great pontiffs – Gregory VII, Innocent III, Boniface VIII, Sixtus V, Pius IX? Certainly, I have no doubt, you have for the great Hildebrand, that heroic combatant, that veritable founder of the Catholic monarchy, the admiration he imposes on everyone. Well, do you know what Cardinal Pietro Damiani, often perplexed by the audacity of his genius, the power of his political combinations, the insatiable ardour of his ambition, called him? He called him "St Satan".'

Abbé Ternisien shivered. He bowed to bid farewell again and walked to the door.

Cardinal Maffeï imperceptibly shrugged his shoulders. With an indifferent eye he saw the former private secretary of Monseigneur de Roquebrun go away, and this time did not think fit to recall him.

XXVI

A CANDIDATE FOR THE PAPACY

Abbé Ternisien died in the first months of 1869. Abbé Lavernède, who had lost his mother more than a year before, being freed from the beloved chain that held him to Lormières, was warned in time, and could come in haste to the Franciscan convent in Tivoli. He had the sad consolation of receiving his friend's last sigh, and of closing his eyes.

As it cannot but happen, the odour of Rome inebriated Lavernède's profoundly Christian soul. Moved and fascinated, he dreamed also of ending his days in this splendid retreat; 'this meeting-place of loving and wounded souls', as Chateaubriand called it. He was on the point of sending his resignation of the chaplaincy of the prisons at Lormières to his bishop – for in spite of Mical, who was less forgetful and more determined, Monseigneur Capdepont had not deigned to remember his former enemy, and had left him in his post – when he received a telegram inviting him to return at once to his diocese and resume the chair of eloquence at the Great Seminary that he had formerly occupied.

What had happened? Nothing more simple. Monseigneur Rufin Capdepont, as Abbé Lavernède himself had foreseen, had pursued his upward progress in the Church and had been made archbishop. The new Bishop of Lormières, Monseigneur Tissandier, anxious to win the affection of his clergy, recalled the diocesan priests to the Great Seminary, having turned out the Jesuits whom Monseigneur Capdepont, wishing to give pleasure at the Gesù, had established there from the beginning of his episcopate.

Monseigneur Capdepont does not give rise to much talk; he lives somewhat retired in his diocese. It is much if, to administer the sacrament of confirmation, he leaves from time to time his archiepiscopal palace, where is kept by work which he will presently publish. People speak covertly of a *History of the Pontificate of Pius IX*, followed by very curious unpublished pieces about the scheming of Cavour and the ministers who followed him: Ricasoli, Ratazzi, Menabrea. This book, which has for an epigraph three Latin words *Crux de cruce*, if we are to believe those who have been allowed to see a few pages, is destined to have the greatest celebrity. All the questions that occupy the religious and political world are faced squarely, and examined with the audacity of genius and, it is said, solved. The absolutist theories of the *Syllabus*, and the new dogma of infallibility, of which Monseigneur Capdepont was one of the most active defenders in the last Council, are (if our information is correct) discussed with a loftiness of view and an abundance of arguments devised, if not to convince the mind, at least to impose admiration for a talent full of suppleness and vigour.

At the moment Monseigneur Capdepont is writing a chapter entitled 'Who Will Be Pius IX's Successor?'

Monseigneur never goes to Paris, where formerly he was often seen. He goes to Rome every year towards the month of May; it is not uncommon for him to go back again in September. The Holy Father gives him a welcome that has aroused jealousy, and the rumour goes round that Pius IX, appreciating the services that a man of the value of Archbishop Rufin renders daily to the Church, and those he may be called upon to render in the future, has privately named him Cardinal. Is it true?

Lately Monseigneur Capdepont was walking with his usual confidant, the Grand Vicar Mical – for Abbé Mical also has seen his ambition satisfied – in the large, beautiful garden that makes a green belt round the archiepiscopal palace.

'Really, Monseigneur, with the way things are going in Italy and Europe, I see in you the future Pope,' the former professor of moral theology said point-blank.

'Do you think so, Mical?'

'I think so, certainly. France has already contributed sixteen

179

successors to St Peter. Why shouldn't you be the seventeenth?'

'May Pius IX have many more years to live! . . . First of all, if the Holy Father were to die, it's the Italian junta that would prevail in the conclave . . .'

'But, Monseigneur, you have only friends in the Sacred College, and the votes might well fall on your eminence.'

'My eminence! . . . Mical, several times I've forbidden you to give me this title.'

The Grand Vicar, whose nose has grown still longer with the years, made a face. Then, having searched the garden paths with his ferrety eyes, he murmured: 'We're alone.'

There was a seat in the shade of the lime trees. The Archbishop sat down . . . he seemed out of breath. Suddenly his head, too heavy with the load of thought, fell on his chest . . . he remained absorbed for a long time.

Mical, as alert as ever and lively as we have always known him, went on: 'I know that Pius IX is very fond of Cardinal de Angelis, Archbishop of Fermo.'

'Sixtus V was Archbishop of Fermo,' murmured Capdepont, not so much answering Mical as the intimate preoccupations of his own mind.

'Yes,' continued the Grand Vicar. 'Cardinal de Angelis could be elected if, as they say, the election should take place before the body of the dead Pope, *ante* . . .'

'No, no!' cried the Archbishop with fire.

A silence of some minutes.

Mical went on: 'Prussia, whose affairs, unfortunately for us, have reached such prosperity, could well use and abuse the position that events have made for her, and put forward the Cardinal Hohenlohe?'

'A German pope! . . . Memories of the long wars of the Papacy and the Empire are still living in the Church. . . . It's impossible. With a German pope one must erase France from the map of the world, which God will not permit. What, France to disappear! As soon see the sun fall from Heaven, and all the nations of the earth flow back to night.'

'But, Monseigneur, what do you think of Cardinal Bonaparte?'

'The name has become suspect in the religious as in the political world. The Cardinal Bonaparte, in spite of his virtues, which one should respect, would not get two votes if he had pretensions to raise himself to the pontifical throne.'

'And the Archbishop of Westminster?'

'Cardinal Manning? . . . If the Holy Father, robbed by the bandits of Savoy, had accepted the hospitality England offered him at Malta, the gratitude of the Sacred College, sheltered from persecution, might have given the Archbishop of Westminster a chance. But the noble obstinacy of Pius IX, who would not leave Rome when it was again invaded by barbarians of the North, leaves no hope to that candidature.'

Harassed by these thoughts, which stabbed him like daggers, the Archbishop rose and, taking the Grand Vicar with him, walked in crazy steps down the darker paths of his garden. His hands, which gripped Mical like claws, were burning. Evidently Capdepont had a fever. His eyes, where all his soul shone, blazed in the shade like so many live coals. He stammered broken words. 'The tiara!' he repeated several times. 'The tiara!'

'Your head, where the power of God placed all the power of faith and genius, would be strong enough to support it.'

Rufin Capdepont stopped short. He gave a long look at the Grand Vicar. Then with the five fingers of his right hand he wiped his forehead, where an ambition close to delirium had lighted the flames of a fearful fire. 'Mical, do you want to drive me mad?' he stammered distractedly. Then with a flash of good sense, and profound humility: 'I, born in a hovel in the hamlet of Harros, I might ascend the steps of the pontifical throne! . . . I, a sinner – you know, I've often sinned in your presence, *malum coram te feci*, as King David said – I could become the Vicar of Jesus Christ on earth! . . . And what have I done to deserve that?' He paused, and then continued: 'I'm the victim of a horrible dream. . . . And if . . . ah, the Catholic world would see a pope, then!'

'God raised you up for the salvation of all.'

'Mical, I think I'm dying . . . I beg you, shut up, shut up!'

This prayer, made almost with tears, shook the professor of moral theology, who did not dare add a word.

The went back to the palace, but now they walked slowly. Capdepont even stopped from time to time, overcome and immobilized by the terrible pain that he suffered. 'There can be no doubt', he murmured, standing in the middle of a path, 'that Germany and Italy are in league to exercise a decisive influence on the next conclave. This question of Pius IX's successor is a question of life and death for the poor Kingdom of Italy, so pitiful and destitute and wretched. . . . The work of Count Cavour is like a booth at a fair, made of planks of deal, and it would need the strong hand of Bismarck to lay the first stone of a building. . . . Bismarck – ah, there's a man I'd like to cross swords with! . . . In his discourse on the first decade of Livy, Machiavelli declares that at all times the Church has been the obstacle to the political union of Italy. The Church will still be that obstacle! . . . But in the face of German and Italian intrigue what will France do? . . . Suppose as a result of the vexations to which it can't help being exposed, or to a revolution – which is always threatening Europe the Sacred College passed the Alps and took refuge with us? . . . Then . . . the French influence would have a good chance, and my candidature might be put forward. . . . They would act.'

'And you would be elected, Monseigneur.'

'Elected! Elected!'

'After this result, so important to the Church, so glorious for France, your holiness won't refuse me a mitre, I think?'

He did not answer.

They resumed their walk.

While going up the steps of his palace, Rufin Capdepont made another halt. Then, succumbing again to the irresistible fascination of his dream, 'Who knows!' he murmured, raising his arms, 'Who knows!'